I0638083

UNTIL DEATH

DELANEY DIAMOND

GARDEN AVENUE PRESS

1

_____

Predawn, her soft body pressed against his under the covers. She moaned, and he took that sound as an invitation. Pushing up against her backside, he spread his fingers over her soft tummy, and she giggled and slapped his hand.

"Don't you dare," she warned. "You've already worn me out for the morning."

Cruz pressed his lips against the curve at the side of her neck. "I have a lot of energy," he whispered.

"I know. That's why I'm warning you."

He heard the smile in her voice and smiled, too. Then he pulled her tighter against his body, enjoying the closeness they shared—the sweet, enticing scent of her skin and hair, and the comfort of having someone to wake up to in the morning. He simulated sex against her bottom by thrusting his hips forward and backward. She started laughing, and because she laughed he continued to do it, because her happiness was more important to him than anything else in the world.

But then the laughter faded, and she faded. He stopped thrusting as his arms became empty. He could no longer feel her, and his heart started beating fast. He grabbed at her but clutched empty air. Why *couldn't he feel her anymore? As panic grabbed him by the throat, he stretched his arms in vain to hold onto her. She was disappearing right before his eyes, the laughter distant and the sight of her almost gone.*

No.

He couldn't get the word out. It lodged at the base of his throat, like a wayward golf ball, shutting off his air and choking the life from him.

No.

He couldn't let her go. He couldn't.

His heart battered his ribs and his grasping hands became more frantic, but he couldn't reach her, couldn't hold onto her.

She was fading, fading...

Cruz's eyes flew open. Every muscle in his body was clenched tight, the thin sheets wrapped around his thighs, and the fingers of his right hand curled into the mattress beside him. He hauled air into his lungs and tried to calm his racing heart.

The phone ringing had pulled him from his nightmare. It rang two more times but he didn't answer, letting it go to voice-mail because he already knew who was calling by the unique ring tone. Miles. And he didn't want to talk to him.

Cruz stared up at the ceiling in the dark room. The last time he'd been in this apartment had been with Shanice, when she'd told him everything she knew about the missing data and the death of her friend. She'd taken the chance and shared the information with him, despite her original fears that he could no more be trusted than the deadly assassins who were after her.

With stark wakefulness, he faced the grim reality that Shanice wasn't there. The nightmare was not a dream, but his present. Someone had removed her from his life, the best thing that had happened to him...ever. The spot where she should be sleeping beside him on the bed was cold and empty, because she was gone for good.

Cruz relaxed his tense body and ran a hand over his hard, aching dick and groaned.

The past four weeks had been difficult—with the agony of loss consuming him—but his mission had made them bearable. Nancy Cheng, the director of Plan B, had offered the agency's services to help him find out who'd blown up his house and killed Shanice, but he'd turned her down. They'd done enough by confirming through DNA analysis that the fragments of human remains uncovered at the scene had been her. Focusing on retribution kept him driven and energized. All of his hard work would pay off tonight, and if he didn't get the answers he wanted, he'd simply dispose of the men and keep searching until he got the answers to his questions.

He tossed aside the sheet and rolled out of bed. Dropping to the floor, he brought his heart rate back up and primed his muscles by doing fifty one-handed pushups on each arm. Then he dressed in silence, tugging on a pair of jeans and a vintage blue T-shirt with a skull and crossbones on the front. He slipped heavy boots onto his feet and then washed his face in the bathroom.

When he finished, he checked his appearance in the mirror and passed a comb through his too long black hair and the whiskers on his jaw. He hadn't shaved or had a haircut in weeks, caring little about his appearance for the time being.

He then stepped out of the bathroom and picked up a small duffel bag on the desk against the wall, casting a cursory glance over the interior of the studio apartment because he didn't know when he'd be back. Satisfied, he grabbed his keys and left.

Time to get to work.

CRUZ SAT with his elbow resting on the open window of a rented charcoal-gray SUV in the gravel and dirt-covered parking lot of Peter's Bar. The seedy-looking spot on the outskirts of Miami was filled with cars from patrons coming and going every few minutes. Loud rock music poured from the inside each time someone entered or exited the building. From this location, he had a good view of the entrance and knew the men he was waiting for would arrive shortly. He'd watched them for a while and knew their routine. All he had to do was wait, and he'd get them both at the same time.

As expected, they arrived together in an older model gray pickup and parked a couple of cars over. His eyes narrowed as he watched them approach the door.

The first was Tony Ortiz, five foot ten with dark hair and a wiry build. Highly skilled, if you considered that he was a demolitions expert with a construction company. His knowledge of explosives meant he had the expertise to obliterate a building without destroying surrounding structures.

His brother, Edgar, followed behind him and was about the same height but with sandy-blond hair and a stocky build. He was a mechanic at a Honda dealership and had a short rap sheet of offenses from his youth. The usual dumb shit like vandalism, fighting, and underage drinking.

These were the jokers he'd seen drive out of his neighborhood in Islamorada the day his house had been blown to smithereens with Shanice inside. He swallowed past the lump in his throat as renewed grief and anger overcame him.

It hadn't taken him long to find them because they were clearly amateurs, wannabe thugs who had been dumb enough to drive into Cruz's neighborhood in a two-door Honda Civic a customer brought in for repairs to the dealership where Edgar worked. They'd had enough sense to swap the license plates, but used the plate from another vehicle on the lot. Not so smart, and easy to trace.

Cruz's gaze followed them as they entered the bar, talking and grinning from ear to ear, unaware he'd been watching them for two weeks. Once Cruz tracked down Edgar, he was led to Tony in short order. After that, he simply used the patience of surveillance to find out where Tony worked, where they both lived, and who were the people they cared about. He also learned they loved to drink at Peter's Bar and hit the spot three nights a week, especially hard on Friday nights.

Tonight was Friday night.

Cruz rolled up the window and picked up a roll of quarters from the console and stuck them in his pants pocket when he exited the SUV. He hadn't always entered the bar during his surveillance, but he hadn't eaten since lunch and was hungry. Might as well get a bite to eat while he was there.

He entered the gloomy bar and quickly assessed the interior like he'd done several times before. The place smelled like hot wings, beer, and sweat, and in addition to the loud music, there was loud talking from the mostly male clientele. Through an open door, he saw a group of men playing pool, yelling and trashing each other over the table. His gaze landed on the brothers seated on two wooden stools in front of the bar. Now that he had them in sight, he scanned the room to find a spot where he could keep an eye on them.

No one paid him any mind as he sauntered to a corner, deep in the shadows so he wouldn't draw attention to himself. Not easy to do with a man of his size, but he learned long ago to blend into the background. He sat on a plain wood chair at the plain wood table, and from this vantage point had a view of the bar where the brothers sat yakking it up with the Dominican bartender and other customers.

The waitress came over, chewing gum, and flicked her gaze over Cruz. He recognized her from one of the other nights he had been there. She wore false lashes that were too long and her dark hair pulled back into a short ponytail.

"Hi, I'm Tina. I'll be your server tonight. What can I get for you, *papi*?" She popped her gum and pulled a pad and pencil from the pocket of her apron.

"Whiskey, straight up, then a root beer with your largest hamburger and two orders of fries."

"Two?"

Cruz nodded.

The waitress scribbled down the words. "Cheese on that burger?" she asked.

"Sure, why not?" He flashed a disarming smile, and she smiled back.

"Coming right up, big boy."

She walked away with her hips swaying and looked over her shoulder to make sure he was still watching. He flicked his gaze away before she could see that he had been watching because he didn't want her to think that he was interested.

Cruz widened his legs and sat back in the chair. The bar would be filled to capacity soon, with people anxious to burn through their paychecks. The brothers worked on beers and a basket of wings each. He knew that this was just the beginning for them. They would be there for at least another two hours.

But he had nothing better to do than wait. He no longer had a job ever since he had left his position at Plan B. He no longer had a woman, because someone had taken her life and destroyed his in the process. It took a lot of willpower not to charge over there and bash their skulls against the bar top for what they had done, because he was certain these were the men who had killed Shanice.

He had every intention of killing them. But first, he needed to find out who had sent them.

2

The Ortiz brothers were on their feet, with Edgar handing a credit card to the bartender.

Cruz had already asked for the bill, which was next to his half-eaten second serving of fries. While the brothers finished paying their tab, he dropped cash on the table. Tina was taking an order from two men nearby. He flashed her a brief smile, which she returned, and then he headed toward the door.

On the way, he took the roll of coins from his pocket and enclosed them in a tight fist, an old street-fighting trick to increase the force and velocity of a punch. The coins also protected the fragile bones of the hand. Though Cruz's had been thickened and toughened from years of use, he still found the technique helpful.

When the brothers finally came out, he was leaning against a white Neon next to their gray pickup. At the same time, a man and woman stepped out of their car, which meant he had to stall because he couldn't move on them until the couple left.

Tony approached the driver's side, where Cruz stood.

"Hey, man." He nodded at Cruz, looking curious but unconcerned. The drinking and boisterous atmosphere of the bar still had him in a relaxed mood.

"Hey, don't I know you?" Cruz frowned, as if trying to remember where he knew him from, at the same time watching the couple from the corner of his eye as they approached the bar's door.

Tony frowned. "Nah, man, you don't know me."

His brother watched the exchange from the passenger side of the truck.

"Yeah, I know you," Cruz said.

"Where you think you know me from?" Tony asked suspiciously.

Edgar came around the front of the vehicle, squaring his shoulders and puffing his chest out in an effort to appear bigger and more intimidating. "Listen *hombre*, you don't want none of this. Find some other sucker to rob." He lifted the front of his T-shirt to show the Glock stuck in his waistband.

Experience had taught Cruz that most people who flashed a piece and didn't pull it out, weren't ready to use it, which made their reaction time slow. Edgar's would be even slower because he'd been drinking.

The couple entered the bar, and Cruz's eyes hardened as he straightened to his full six feet five inches. "You murdered my girlfriend," he said.

"What?" Tony laughed and shot a glance at his brother. "We never murdered anyone. Who the fuck are you, anyway?"

"I'm the man who's going to kill you." Cruz grinned.

Tony laughed again, uneasily this time, and looked at his brother who was clearly the leader and more aggressive one.

"Oh yeah?" Edgar said.

"Yeah," Cruz answered.

He slammed his left fist into Tony's jaw, knocking him sideways. He fell hard onto the gravel.

He swung toward Edgar, who was reaching for the gun,

but Cruz grabbed his wrist and twisted his arm. The older brother yelled out and Cruz punched him in the stomach with the coin-wrapped fist, forcing a gust of air from his mouth as he squinted and doubled over in pain. Then Cruz slammed his head against the Neon's door, knocking him out cold.

Cruz removed the gun from his waistband, and Tony, who was still on the ground, raised up on one hand and lifted the other in a pleading motion. "Come on, man, you got the wrong people. We didn't kill nobody, I swear."

"Get up."

Tony's gaze shifted to his unconscious brother, then he stood carefully with his hands raised in a display of surrender. A red bruise swathed his right cheek. It must hurt like hell. He was about to hurt a lot more.

"Don't kill us, man. I swear, we don't know nothing about your girlfriend."

"*Cállate la boca.*" Cruz popped the side of his head with a back-handed blow of the weapon, and he fell to the ground.

He stuck the gun in his back waistband under his T-shirt and then carried Tony to the SUV two cars over and tossed him in the trunk. The sound of rock music filled the air, and Cruz watched through the front windshield as two men left the bar and came straight toward them.

He hurried over to where Edgar lay and scooped him up under the arms.

One of the men pulled up short. "Goddamn. What happened to him?"

Cruz shook his head, pasting an expression of sadness on his face. "Can't hold his liquor. Gotta take him home so his wife doesn't kill him."

"Wasn't he with another guy? His brother, I thought?" the other man asked.

"Yeah, he caught a cab home." Cruz laughed and shook his

head again. "Drunk fool left his brother behind. Can you believe that? Eddie's going to kick his ass tomorrow."

"I know I would."

The men laughed and walked away.

Cruz pretended to struggle with Edgar until they had driven out of the parking lot. Then he hoisted him over his shoulder and moved swiftly before anyone else came along. He tossed him in the back with his younger brother and zip-tied their hands and feet together.

Then he slammed the trunk closed and left the parking lot.

AN ABANDONED WAREHOUSE PROVIDED the isolation Cruz needed to get information from the brothers, and an opportunity to easily dispose of their bodies when he was done.

While they were both still unconscious, he'd tied each of them to chairs bolted to the floor, but he'd thought for sure they'd be awake by now. He smacked one and then the other, multiple times on their cheeks. As they regained consciousness, their heads lolled on their necks before they gazed around at their surroundings in confusion. Cruz silently looked down at them, getting a perverse sense of satisfaction at the fear that entered their eyes when they saw they were in a warehouse and realized they were tied up.

"Who are you, man?" Tony asked, voice wavering. He was the weaker link.

"I'll be the one asking the questions. Question number one, who sent you to blow up the house in Islamorada about a month ago?"

"We don't know what you're talking about," Edgar said, defiance in the set of his chin and hardening of his dark eyes.

Cruz took his time looking from one to the other. "I'm not here to play games with the two of you. I don't play games. I'm going to ask you again, and this is the last time I'm going to ask. Who sent you to blow up the house in Islamorada?"

"Same answer. We don't know what you're talking about."

Cruz walked over to a chair facing the brothers and picked up a large envelope. He sat down, resting an ankle on one knee. "You don't know anything, eh?" He pulled out a bunch of photographs he had developed. "That was my house you blew up. My home, with my woman inside."

Tony's eyes widened. "There was no one inside the house!" he blurted.

Cruz paused, insides tightening at the incriminating words.

"Man, shut up!" his brother growled at him.

Tony shrank in the chair, his face turning red.

"So, you do know about the house," Cruz said slowly. "Just like I know all about *your* houses."

He tossed a couple of the photos to the cement floor in front of their feet. They spun and landed haphazardly, but it would be obvious to the brothers that those photos were of their homes. They showed a group of townhouses where they lived a few doors down from each other, their house numbers clearly visible in gold beside each door.

"*Mira aquí*, I even know what car you drive."

He tossed down more photos. These showed Tony pumping gas and another of him getting into the vehicle with a sack of groceries. More photos were thrown to the ground that showed a behind-the-car shot of Edgar's vehicle, his license plate number visible. Other shots showed the brothers in various locations around the city in their cars as they ran errands, went to work, and went to the bar.

Edgar's lips tightened.

Tony's eyes widened. "How long have you been following us?" he asked, voice ending on a squeak.

"Long enough to know where your parents live." Cruz tossed two photos to the growing pile. "Long enough to know that Edgar's wife works at the Publix on 27th." More photos tossed down.

"You leave my wife out of this! You leave my family out of this!" Edgar jerked against the restraints, face turning crimson and the veins in his neck popping against his skin.

Cruz looked calmly at him. Edgar was completely restrained, and there was no way he could get loose. "I know everything about you *pendejos*, and since you won't talk, maybe I'll go pay your families a visit. Maybe they can answer my questions. I'll be right back."

Sometimes the fastest way to get information was to threaten the life or safety of a loved one. Some people could hold out for long periods, even indefinitely if they were only concerned about harm to themselves. But factor in harm to someone they loved, and they became a fountain of information, often providing details you didn't ask for. It was an emotional response, and an emotional response could mean the difference between spending minutes or hours working over an asset.

He stood and started toward the exit as if he were about to leave.

"No, wait!" Tony yelled.

"Don't tell him shit," Edgar growled.

Cruz turned slowly, narrowing his eyes. Edgar was really starting to piss him off with all his bravado. Some people were too dumb to realize when they were outmatched.

"This is really how you want to handle the situation, as if you have the upper hand?" Cruz asked.

He snatched the gun from the back of his waistband and watched with satisfaction as Edgar's eyes widened. "Since you don't want to talk, but your brother will, I'll get rid of you right now."

Tony's panicked gaze jumped from Cruz to Edgar and back again. "Don't kill him. I'll tell you anything you want to know."

"I'm done being nice," Cruz said in a steely voice. He walked over to Edgar and grabbed a handful of his hair. "Open your mouth."

Edgar shook his head, blatant fear now filling his eyes. He pulled his lips in, tightening them as if that would stop Cruz.

"I said open your goddamn mouth!" Cruz snarled.

Tightening his fingers in Edgar's hair, he yanked back his head and forced the gun hard against his lips. "Open your mouth or I'll bust out all your teeth."

Edgar whimpered, but seconds later, his mouth opened. Cruz stuck in the gun and stared into Edgar's eyes. "Don't think for one minute I won't blow your fucking head off. The only thing keeping you alive is that I want information. But if your brother can't, or won't, give me the answers I want within the next sixty seconds, I'm pulling the trigger and putting a hole in the back of your fucking skull—*¿comprendes cabrón?*"

"No, wait, don't kill me. Please don't kill me!" Edgar's attitude had changed. His muffled words were spoken around the barrel of the gun but still understood. His eyes filled with tears as he pleaded for his life.

"I'll tell you anything you want to know." Tony yanked in vain against the restraints.

Cruz had purposely picked Edgar's mouth to shove the gun into—not only because he got on his nerves, but because he was the one with the rap sheet, and Tony would be easier to break. Tony wasn't used to this life, and Edgar's bravado meant wasting time Cruz didn't want to waste.

He turned his head slowly to look at Tony, leaving the gun perched in his brother's mouth. "Who hired you?" he demanded.

"I-I don't know. We don't know. W-we didn't get a name. A friend of ours told us that someone needed the job done. H-he knew that I work in demolition and thought I would be perfect. Said it would be easy money. We got half up front, a-and when the job was done the rest of the money was wired into our accounts."

"I don't believe you." Cruz kept his voice even, emotionless.

"I told you the truth, I swear! That's everything that I know, man. We were trying to make a quick buck, that's all."

"In your effort to make a quick buck, an innocent woman was killed." Cruz felt the darkness of anger creeping over him again and fought back the urge to smash and hurt and maim.

"They told us the house was empty."

"It wasn't empty."

Tears streamed down Tony's face now. "We woulda never done it if we knew someone was g-going to die, man. Honest to God." His eyes darted between Cruz and the gun stuck in his brother's mouth.

He seemed to be telling the truth. But if he was telling the truth, that would mean...

What if...?

Cruz removed the gun and stepped back, mind reeling with the possibilities as he assessed everything he knew.

Emotion. Wicked, chaotic emotion had to be removed so he could think clearly.

The first days after the explosion, he'd been numb and in disbelief. Since then, he'd been consumed with revenge, certain Shanice had been murdered by someone who wanted to get at him. Perhaps punish him. An old enemy, potentially the result of any number of cases from the past. But now, he wondered.

These fools probably truly had no idea who had paid them. They were nothing but small-time hustlers looking for a quick buck, like Tony said.

He took in Tony's tear-streaked face and Edgar's much more somber expression, the result of the metallic taste of the gun—an instrument that could take his life in a split second—lingering on his tongue.

Cruz needed time to think. He went behind Tony's chair and untied him. Then he untied Edgar.

Both men stood slowly, looking at him, rubbing their bruised wrists where the rope had chafed their skin.

Cruz held the gun at his side but didn't point it at them. It was enough for them to see him holding it. "Don't do something stupid and go to the cops about what happened tonight, and stay out of trouble. If I find out that you haven't obeyed what I just said, I'm coming for you and your family, and next time, I won't be so nice."

He dipped his gaze to the pictures on the floor, and they followed suit. He wasn't so low that he'd go after their family. His beef was with them, but he'd let them think he would so they'd stay in line.

Tony gulped, perhaps realizing that not only was their family in danger, but they themselves had been in danger for a while and unaware of it.

"Get out of here," Cruz said.

Their heads snapped up. They looked at each other and then darted toward the open doorway as if a family of alligators were nipping at their heels.

Cruz stuck Edgar's weapon back in his waistband and gathered up the photos. He tucked them in the envelope and left the scene.

He had somewhere to go, too.

3

Shanice aimed at the paper target and counted in her head. One. Two. Three. She squeezed the trigger. The gun jerked in her hand and she clipped the edge of the paper, wincing at the loud noise. Thank goodness for the air plugs.

She'd been coming here for two weeks and still hadn't gotten used to the recoil and loud bang. The last time she'd fired a gun had been with her father, when she'd been a teenager. He'd wanted her to get comfortable with guns, but she'd never actually been able to. They were too loud and the thought of hurting someone turned her stomach.

She lowered the muzzle, aimed for center mass, and fired again. A hot casing popped up and hit her safety goggles, and the bullet landed on the upper right of the paper.

"Come on," she muttered in frustration.

Concentrating, she adjusted the position of the gun and tried again. The last bullet hit closer to the center of the scoring rings, but still wasn't good enough. *Crap.*

She wanted to get better. She wanted to be prepared. Her

life had been in danger, and though she'd moved away to safety, needed to be able to protect herself—just in case.

Expect the best, plan for the worst. That's what Cruz always said. *Cruz.*

Overwhelming sadness crushed her chest, and Shanice dropped her hands onto the shelf in front of her. Tears flooded her vision and she stifled a sob. What was she doing here? She turned twenty-nine today and was at the firing range, trying her best not to think about how she had no one to celebrate with, and the man she loved was gone from her life. For good.

Spikes of longing were her constant companion. Cruz was dead. They'd never hold each other again. She'd never kiss him again. Their time together had been short—way too short. The pain turned to anger at the injustice of it all. Firming her lips, she lifted her hands and gripped the handgun. She aimed and fired off three more shots in quick succession. *Bang, bang, bang.* The target fluttered three times.

Shanice lowered her hands to the shelf again. Tired, frustrated, and feeling inexplicably defeated, she was in no condition to practice. With a heavy sigh, she gathered the rounds and gun, which she'd rented from the range, and pulled forward the sheet. Two of the bullets landed near the drawn figure's right shoulder and one in the neck.

She went out to the front of the range.

"How'd it go?" the clerk asked, as he took the gun.

Shanice shrugged. "Better than two weeks ago, I guess," she said with a weak smile.

"Your accuracy will increase, but you gotta keep practicing."

Shanice didn't respond, only nodded her head. She left the range and drove out of the parking lot in her gray Corolla, a car that didn't draw attention. Something else she'd learned from Cruz during their time together.

She gripped the steering wheel tighter. She couldn't stop

thinking about him. Day after day, hour after hour, he consumed her thoughts.

She made a quick stop to pick up a roast beef sandwich for lunch and added a German chocolate cupcake for the celebratory portion of the meal. Something to make herself feel better. Then she headed home, crossing the invisible boundary at the *Welcome to Hopevale* sign.

Hopevale, Georgia was a small city about thirty-five minutes east of Atlanta, consisting of a small but growing downtown, a bustling art and music scene, and dining options that catered to a variety of foodie preferences. It was exactly the kind of place she could be happy living in and had jumped at the chance when the opportunity presented itself.

She drove down Rainbow Street and cruised past houses on either side, some with flowers brightening the front, others with children's bikes and multi-colored toys scattered on the lawns. She pulled her vehicle onto the driveway and past the rotting white picket fence that lined the front of her property. The Victorian-style home was much more house than she needed, but she'd liked it on sight.

It had a front and back porch, and the master bedroom had a private balcony that overlooked the street. The door to the detached garage wasn't working, and the landlord had promised to send someone out to fix it over a week ago. She'd have to remind him to set the appointment. There was a lot of work that needed to be done on the house, but it was home, for now.

"Hello, Mary!" The housewife across the street was watering her lawn and waved.

Shanice waved and smiled back.

Mary was the name of one of her aunts, and she'd chosen the alias when she fled Islamorada. Mary Jones. A simple, generic name.

Shanice rested a hand on her hip. "Hi, Tricia, how's it going?"

"Good. Trying to survive this heat. Fall can't come soon enough for me—make things cool down around here. How are the renovations coming?"

Tricia always complained about the heat and wore a wide-brim hat on her curly red hair. Shanice had never seen her spend much time outside without the hat to protect her pale skin.

"I should be further along," she said with an embarrassed laugh, "but I'm getting there."

After moving in two months ago, there was still so much work to do on the house, but she didn't mind. The work kept her busy, and the landlord had offered a discount on the rent in exchange for the repairs.

"Oh, honey, don't feel bad. That house had been sitting vacant for a long time. I'm sure you have your hands full with it. You're welcome to join us for dinner any time you need a break."

That was the third time she'd made the offer, and though Shanice was tempted to accept, she didn't feel up to the constant lying she'd have to do about her past.

"I'll keep that in mind. Thank you." She waved goodbye and then stepped onto the front porch.

Once inside, she locked the door and took a moment to peer through the blinds over the window. She did that a lot lately—watching, wondering if she were being followed. Nothing had happened so far, but she was always worried that one day a stranger would show up at her door with her name on a death warrant.

Satisfied she hadn't been followed, Shanice walked deeper into the house. There were four spacious bedrooms, a formal dining room, a living room, and a large, eat-in kitchen with a view of the back yard. A week after she moved in, the landlord had bought and delivered black stainless steel appliances that modernized the kitchen and went well with the dove-gray cabinets.

She took a can of soda from the refrigerator and made her way up the stairs. She entered one of the bedrooms, where she'd been spending a lot of time lately, and lowered to the new carpet. There wasn't any furniture in there yet, but that would come later.

She hated that she couldn't tell anyone where she was, not even her mother. The deal was, she had to stay hidden for her own safety, which meant for the second time in her life, she was all alone again. This time with a new identity.

Well, not completely alone, and this arrangement was supposed to only be temporary. Yes, she'd started a new life— one that didn't promise much excitement, except...

She pressed a hand to her stomach and smiled. She was three and a half months pregnant but wasn't showing yet and couldn't wait until she was. She did have cravings, though, especially for pistachio ice cream, for some reason.

Her gaze surveyed the room. Her paint job so far wasn't bad —a nice bright yellow that made the wall glow when the sun came through the windows. When she finished, she'd sticker one wall with the dinosaur and Winnie the Pooh images she had picked up at the local Target. She couldn't decide and had gone with both.

She didn't know if she was having a boy or girl yet, but she was happy to have a piece of Cruz with her always. She would tell her baby about their father and what a great man he was.

"God, Cruz, I wish you were here," she whispered brokenly but refused to cry. Not again. She'd cried plenty in the past couple of months, especially late at night when the loneliness descended and she thought about being a single parent and having to start over with no real friends. "But don't worry, I'm going to make sure our little guy or girl knows all about their brave daddy."

She swiped brown icing off the top of the cake and sucked it off her finger. Her eyes came to rest on a specific spot in the room, and she decided that's where she'd place the crib, and maybe a rocking chair in the corner.

Shanice continued to eat in silence, wishing things could be different. Life had been tough, but in less than six months, they would be a whole lot better.

4

Miles Garrison had been persistent, calling Cruz twice a week since he walked away. *Nancy wants you to do one more job*, he'd said. But Cruz had had zero interest and stopped answering his calls.

He had been obligated to eight years with the organization and passed that point four years ago. As time went by, his desire to work had no longer been out of obligation, but about protecting the country he now called home. He'd channeled the aggression of his youth into more positive avenues, like taking out threats, so others could have the same opportunity he did to obtain the ideals of life, liberty, and the pursuit of happiness.

But that was all in the past. He'd paid his debt and didn't owe anyone anything else. Certainly not the government. So he'd never expected to see Miles again. That changed after he talked to the Ortiz brothers.

Cruz entered Miles's home with ease. He'd been watching the place for over an hour and there didn't seem to be anyone at home.

The front of the townhouse faced the street, so he slipped

in through the back after disarming the alarm. He set his small leather pouch on the counter in the kitchen and waited inside the door until his eyes adjusted to the darkness. Then he walked quietly through the house, down the hall and into the living room, ears pricked and listening for movement within.

After a sweep of the upstairs rooms, he went back downstairs and re-entered the kitchen. There wasn't much in the refrigerator. Beer, kombucha, bottled smoothies, and a container of half-eaten oxtails and rice.

Cruz removed a green smoothie and went to the living room. He set his pouch on the coffee table, dragged one of the chairs against the wall, and sat facing the door. He sat there for almost an hour before he heard the key in the lock. By then, he'd finished the smoothie.

Miles was only a dark shape against the exterior lights as he entered. He shut the door, and Cruz caught the split-second pause as he realized the alarm didn't go off and sensed someone in the room with him. With a swift motion, he turned and planted his feet apart, gun extended.

"Who's there?"

"It's me. Put the gun down."

Miles's position relaxed. "Cruz?"

"Yes." He flicked on the floor lamp nearby.

Miles lowered his gun and stared in disbelief. "I could have killed you."

"You're way too slow. You've gotten soft, and frankly, I could have killed you the minute you walked in the door."

"Yeah, well, you're a maniac. What's with the beard?"

"I'm trying something different." Cruz ran a hand across his jawline, keeping his eyes on Miles.

Miles re-holstered the weapon under his jacket. He was dark-skinned, had a full beard, and was in his late thirties. As usual, he was dressed in a suit, this one black with a black and white striped tie. Frowning, he asked, "What are you doing in my house?"

"We need to talk."

"Mind if I get a drink first? I see you've already helped yourself." Miles nodded toward the empty bottle Cruz had placed on the floor.

Cruz smiled. "I'll be waiting." He didn't know how or if Miles was involved in Shanice's disappearance, so for now, he'd play nice with him.

Shaking his head, Miles disappeared down the hall.

The living room didn't appear to be *lived* in. It contained nice furniture—a purple and yellow striped couch, with the floral equivalent in the two armchairs, one of which Cruz sat in. There was a side table and coffee table, and the lamp. That was it. No photos or paintings on the walls.

Miles returned with a bottle of kombucha.

"You had a ton of that in the fridge," Cruz remarked.

Miles placed his gun on the coffee table, tossed his jacket on the arm of the sofa, and sat down. He took a swig from the bottle and set it on a napkin he'd brought in with him. "It's supposed to be good for you. People have been drinking kombucha for thousands of years. It's supposed to be full of antioxidants and promote good gut health. Shit like that. Aisha got me started drinking it."

Cruz noticed how his jaw hardened under his beard. "When did she leave you?"

Miles let out a sound that was supposed to be a laugh but instead came out like a bitter grunt. "What makes you think she left me?"

"There's no food in the fridge, nothing on the walls, and only men's clothes in the closet in the master bedroom."

"I feel violated." Miles took another drink, clearly avoiding giving a response. Then, as if defeated, he let out a sigh and met Cruz's gaze. "She left a few weeks ago. Our vacation back in March was supposed to be a new start, a way to smooth things over between us. I sensed she was going to leave and the trip bought me a little more time, but...she left anyway."

"Because of the job?"

"Yeah," Miles replied in a crushed voice. "She got tired. That's what she said. She was just...tired. I told her it could be worse, that she could be married to a man like my father, who used my mother as a punching bag. That didn't seem to change her mind. I can save the country, but I couldn't save my goddamn marriage."

"I'm sorry."

He shrugged. "It is what it is. She hasn't filed for divorce yet, but it's coming. She can have anything she wants, but my kid..." He shook his head. "That's nonnegotiable."

Miles and Aisha had struggled to get pregnant, and their little girl was a bright spot in Miles's life. No matter what difficulties occurred in his marriage, he couldn't help but smile when he discussed his daughter—his miracle, as he called her —so it was no surprise that he'd fight tooth and nail to keep her in his life.

"You didn't break into my house to talk about my marital problems. You ready to come back to the agency?"

"That's what I came to talk to you about—the agency." Cruz leaned forward, elbows to knees. He watched Miles closely as he said the next words. "I believe Shanice is alive."

Miles reared back. "What?" His expression looked like genuine surprise, but that didn't mean he wasn't faking.

"You heard me. I tracked down the men who blew up my house, and I questioned them."

Miles quirked an eyebrow.

"They swear they knew nothing about Shanice being in the house, and that they were only instructed to blow up the place."

"That's what they *said*. Doesn't mean they're telling the truth."

Cruz sat back. "I believe them."

"Still doesn't mean she wasn't in the house. You want to believe Shanice is still alive. There was a body—"

"No!" Cruz cut him off with a growl and felt his face distort into fury. "I've thought about the circumstances surrounding what I *thought* was her death, and I have doubts."

"The DNA analysis confirmed that it was her," Miles said slowly, carefully, as if trying to calm an enraged lunatic.

"I don't believe that anymore. I don't know that was her body in there, and the idea that someone was trying to get at me through her doesn't make sense. If that's the case, why haven't they come forward to claim responsibility? To gloat?"

"Cruz, listen to me. You're not an emotional person, but you loved this woman, and your relationship has thrown you for a loop. I get it. Love can mess you up. People do crazy things for love and behave in ways they wouldn't normally, because of that goddamn emotion. Even someone as trained as you. It stands to reason that...that maybe you want her to be alive when she really isn't." Miles's voice gentled, going softer on the last part of the sentence. "You're not thinking clearly."

Cruz glared at him. "I wasn't thinking clearly *before*, but now I am. It's as if someone removed a blindfold and I can see the truth, without emotion fucking with my head."

"All right, fine." Miles threw up his hands. "If she's not dead, then give me one good reason why someone would want you to think she was dead and not claim responsibility."

"Only one answer makes sense. Because if she'd simply disappeared, they knew I wouldn't have rested until I found her. They didn't want me to go looking for her, so they made me think she was dead. Why? I wanted to leave Plan B because of her. If she's dead, then I'd return—or so that person thought.

They didn't anticipate that I'd still walk away." He let the words hang in the air as he looked steadily across at Miles.

Awareness dawned in Miles's eyes, and his eyes widened in panic.

He lunged for the gun on the table, but Cruz snatched it up first and both men jumped to their feet.

Miles flung his hands in the air.

"What the hell did you do?" Cruz asked.

Miles swallowed hard. "Cruz, you're wrong about me. I didn't have anything to do with Shanice's disappearance. I swear!"

"She hadn't been dead a week before you started calling me, asking if I'd like to come back to do one more job."

"Because I thought the job would take your mind off losing your woman and having your house blown up. I was trying to be a friend to you."

"Bullshit! Where is she?"

"I don't know!" Miles yelled. He closed his eyes and when he opened them again, he appeared calmer. "I had no reason to get rid of Shanice. I wanted you to remain at Plan B, yes, but I wouldn't do anything so low as to destroy your home and make you think your woman was dead when she wasn't. I actually thought she might be good for you. Make you a little more human. I had *nothing* to do with her disappearance."

"How do I know you're telling me the truth?"

"You don't, but all I can tell you is that I wouldn't do that. But we both know who would—who's capable of greenlighting that type of action, falsifying evidence, and keeping the entire operation quiet."

They both stared at each other, and Cruz lowered the gun.

"Nancy," they both said.

5

Two months ago

Shanice left the doctor's office with a smile on her face.
Walking down the sidewalk, she cradled her belly, imagining what the life inside her would look like. Would her baby look more like their father, Cruz? Would they have his umber eyes and intensity? Or would they be like her—more sensitive, with brown eyes?

Whatever their baby looked like, even if he or she was a combination of both parents, she was excited about the prospect. She was surprisingly excited, considering she didn't know Cruz's thoughts about children and starting a family together.

Shanice was about to step off the sidewalk when two people wearing suits came up to her—a tall Black woman with blonde hair and a square-jawed man who reminded her of Cruz because of his height, tawny skin, and muscular build under his clothes.

"Miss Lawrence?" the woman said.

Shanice hesitated, eyeing them with distrust. They were a

bit intimidating, both tall and wearing dark sunglasses so she couldn't see their eyes.

"Who's asking?" She inserted her hand into her large purse, closing her fingers around the pepper spray Cruz had bought for her a while back.

"We need you to come with us, please," the blonde said.

Shanice took a step back and scanned the parking lot, recalling Cruz's words. *Always pay attention to your surroundings. Find the exit routes and avenues for escape should you need them.*

"Look, I don't know who you are or what you want, but I'm not going anywhere with you."

"We know Cruz, and we have someone who wants to speak to you about him." The man spoke in the same monotone voice as the blonde.

When they mentioned Cruz's name, her ears perked up. "Where is this person?"

A black sedan with dark windows idled near the curb. She guessed the person or persons in the vehicle was with these two. If necessary, she could rush back to the front door of the building and get help. Otherwise, there wasn't much to see in the small lot filled with empty cars. There was a ticket booth where exiting vehicles were required to stop and pay for parking, and there was a woman getting her toddler out of a mini-van.

"In the car over there." The blonde nodded to the sedan.

The man spoke next. "We mean you no harm, but what we have to tell you is important."

Shanice hesitated. She didn't know what to do. If they had news about Cruz, she wanted to know. He'd been gone a month already, and she'd only heard from him once, via a postcard that had simply said *Thinking about you*. She'd known it was him because of the handwriting. He'd wanted to send a message to put her mind at ease, which she appreciated.

Shanice stepped back and shook her head. "I'm not getting in that car."

"Please wait here," the man said.

He walked over to the vehicle and tapped the back window. It was rolled down. He spoke to someone on the inside, but she couldn't hear what they were saying.

The woman beside her remained quiet, stoic.

The man nodded, opened the door, and then stepped back. An Asian woman exited the interior wearing a classic Chanel suit in black and peach. Long pearl necklaces dropped as far as her waistline in a variety of lengths.

Her hair was pinned back from her face into a neat bun at her nape. "Miss Lawrence," she said in a smooth, cultured voice, lifting her hand in welcome.

Shanice moved slowly toward her, the blonde at her side.

"I'm Nancy Cheng, the head of the organization Cruz works for."

They shook hands. The woman had a strong grip.

"I promise you, we mean you no harm, but we have vital information to share with you about Cruz, and it's imperative we speak with you in private. Would you join me in the back seat, please?"

Shanice peered inside. There was no one else in the car, which meant one of the other two people was the driver.

"Only if it's you and me in the car, no one else, and I can take out my pepper spray. Excuse me if I'm cautious, but some crazy things have happened to me over the past few months, and I want to be careful."

"*Of course*, I understand. You've been through a traumatic experience. Thank you for joining me." She directed the next words to the man and woman standing nearby. "Please wait here while I speak to Miss Lawrence in private." She slipped into the car.

Shanice joined her and shut the door. She removed her pepper spray and held it in her right hand, just in case.

Nancy clasped her hands on her lap. "As I explained, I work at the same agency Cruz works for. I don't know how much he's told you about the work he does."

"Not much," Shanice admitted. She remained purposely vague. She truly didn't know much about the organization he worked for, but she also didn't want to get him into trouble.

"I'm the director," Nancy explained. "I've overseen Cruz and the other agents for a while now. The agency and its agents are an important aspect of our national security, but the work is dangerous. People in this line of work can't get too close to anyone, for their own safety, and for the safety of the people they're involved with."

"Cruz will protect me," Shanice said with confidence. He'd promised to do that, and he was very good at his job.

"If he were here, I'm sure he would," Nancy said quietly.

The air in the car stilled. Shanice replayed the words in her head, trying to make sense of them. Her fingers clenched the pepper spray, and the muscles in her throat tightened to the point where she barely got the next words out. "Wh-what are you saying?"

Nancy rested her smaller hand on top of Shanice's. Her slender fingers provided little comfort.

"I'm sorry to have to tell you this, but I'm sure you know he was on assignment, and...I can't go into detail, but the enemy got the better of him. Cruz is no longer alive, and as the person closest to him, we had to tell you—"

"No, there must be some mistake." Shanice shook her head adamantly. "He's not dead. He's *not*."

The hand that blanketed hers squeezed in an effort to provide comfort, and Nancy's dark eyes filled with sympathy. "It's been confirmed. There was nothing we could do."

She took a white envelope from a pocket at the back of the

driver's seat and removed photos. She turned over the first one and all Shanice saw was a charred body.

She gasped and turned away in shock, her breathing halting as air froze in her lungs. *No. No. What did they do to him?*

"The enemy sent us these pictures to confirm the kill."

With trembling fingers, Shanice touched her belly. He'd never know about their baby. Their baby would never know him.

"We will protect you and your baby," Nancy said gently.

Shanice's head snapped around to her. "How did you...?"

"We know a lot of things, and of course, you left a medical building where there are three ob-gyn offices. It was easy to figure out."

Nancy put away the photos and opened the console in front of them. She pulled out a box of tissues and handed several to Shanice.

Shanice hadn't even registered she was crying until that moment. She dabbed at her wet cheeks and eyes. "What happens now?"

"Now, we have to protect you. Cruz gave strict instructions on what we should do if anything happened to him, and we're happy to do it."

"Protect me? Why do I need protection?"

"Cruz was trying to take down a dangerous organization when he died. If they figure out who he is and who he loves, they'll come after you. And you have someone else to think about." Nancy's gaze lowered to Shanice's belly.

Shanice couldn't talk for a moment. More tears sprang to her eyes, and she wrapped a protective arm around her waistline. "This is too much. I can't process all of this information."

"And you shouldn't have to. Leave the planning to us, but we have to move soon and quickly. We can make you disappear —give you a new identity and help you start over."

Shanice felt sick. She didn't want to start over. She wanted

Cruz and the life he promised. She wanted them to raise their baby together. She wanted him to start that business he'd talked about. There was so much she wanted, and none of it involved disappearing and taking on a new identity.

But what choice did she have? She didn't only have herself to worry about. She had a baby to take care of and protect. And for Cruz's sake, she'd do her best to raise their child, knowing what an amazing father they had. A true American hero.

She faced Nancy. "What's the plan?"

"You'll go into hiding until we apprehend the people who could harm you."

"For how long?"

"Could be a year, could be five years. We don't know. These people are conniving and dangerous, and we don't know when we'll capture them. Because of that, you can't have contact with family and friends."

"My mother—"

"No family at all while you're underground."

Nancy's voice had firmed, and Shanice nodded. She understood the reason for cutting off all contact, though she didn't like it. It was the best way to protect herself, her baby, and her friends and family.

Shanice dabbed at her eyes and took a trembling breath. "Okay," she whispered.

BLINDED BY TEARS, Shanice recalled the last time she'd had to pack in a rush. Cruz had been with her then, and she laughed through the tears, thinking about how afraid she'd been of him and the situation—wondering if they would make it out of Beatrice's house alive.

That all seemed so long ago.

She packed up all of her belongings. There wasn't much.

She took a few things that belonged to Cruz—a couple of his beloved T-shirts, a Panama hat he told her he'd won in a dominoes game, and photos of them she'd had framed and placed around the house. She particularly liked the shot of them dancing on the patio of a restaurant in Key West. A friend had taken the photo, and she remembered that night vividly. She'd teased Cruz, telling him she was surprised how light he was on his feet. He'd warned her not to tell anyone he liked to dance. They were gazing at each other, both looking happy and carefree as they laughed under the stars.

Her heart twisted painfully, and she tucked the photo into the bag on her shoulder.

Shanice cast one more glance at the bedroom they'd shared. The large bed was made now, but she'd woken up several mornings, wrapped in his strong arms, knowing nothing could harm her while he was near. With a bittersweet smile, she shook her head. He wasn't alive, but somehow he'd managed to make sure that she would be safe anyway.

She dragged her suitcases behind her and met the waiting agents in the living room.

"Is that everything?" the female agent asked.

Biting her bottom lip to keep it from trembling, Shanice simply nodded because she couldn't speak. This was it. She had to disappear. She'd already said goodbye to her mother, other family, and friends and explained she couldn't tell them where she was going—for their own protection.

The male agent took the suitcases, and Shanice resettled the bag on her shoulder. They hadn't given her a new name yet or told her where she was going, but she trusted that they would take good care of her. If Cruz had trusted them, she trusted them.

Shanice followed them out the door, her heart breaking, but ready for the new life that awaited her.

6

———

Nancy had a routine, one that was easy enough to learn after only a few days. Pretty careless of her, but that worked to Cruz's advantage.

Every morning at five a.m., her female driver and one bodyguard picked her up and took her to the gym. She wore her workout clothes and tennis shoes, and the driver took her work clothes and heels and carefully laid them in the trunk, while the bodyguard opened the back door so she could climb in. The trio then went to Fit Body Gyms, where Nancy worked out for an hour, while they waited in the parking lot. When she finished, the driver, a Black woman with short blonde hair, pulled up to the front of the building, Nancy climbed in, and the woman drove to Starbucks for her morning coffee. After that, they headed into the office—in plenty of time for Nancy to shower and change and be seated behind her desk by eight o'clock.

Cruz planned to grab her after her workout.

He was dealing with professionals, so he had to be careful, and each day for the past few days he'd followed her using different vehicles. Yesterday he pulled together a plan and everything he needed. Today he sat in the parking lot of the building across the street in an unmarked white van he'd purchased for cash at a used car lot the day before. The vehicle had a lot of miles on it and the seats were stained and worn, but it was sturdy and the engine turned over when he twisted the key in the ignition.

Cruz sipped coffee and watched the building, the front covered mostly in glass so passersby could watch the members exercise, and vice versa. He lifted a monocular to his eye and watched Nancy's progress. Though he hadn't seen her, he suspected she lifted weights during the first part of the routine, then came in front of the second-floor window and used the treadmill. There were earbuds in her ears, connected to her phone resting on top of the machine. In a neon top and black tights, her legs moved swiftly on a sharp incline. Her arms pumped hard and sweat poured down her face. She was nearing the end of her workout. In a few minutes she'd be finished and he'd be ready.

Cruz chose this time and location for several reasons. A former assassin herself, Nancy was no pushover, but after an hour-long workout, she'd be tired and her reflexes dulled. Second, there were fewer people around and little traffic, which meant an easy getaway and few witnesses. If he timed it right, he could grab her at the edge of the parking lot, out of view of most of the gym patrons. Best of all, the abduction was unexpected.

Cruz shoved the last bit of his ham and egg sandwich in his mouth and tossed the crushed paper next to the sledgehammer on the passenger seat. Then he swallowed the last of the coffee and rotated his shoulders and neck muscles, preparing for the confrontation.

When Nancy finished her exercise, Cruz started the van

and the engine hummed to life. During moments like this, nothing could distract him. It was like he had tunnel vision, and all that mattered was the task at hand, which he'd planned down to the finest detail, including contingencies in case everything didn't go as he wanted.

He was never satisfied with perfection. He always wanted to surpass perfection—to be better than the best. As a boy, his mother used to tell him, "You're so intense."

He was no longer that intense little boy obsessed with perfection. Now he was a man obsessed with perfection, and his instincts were sharper and his body stronger. He was going to use those assets to grab the person keeping him from the woman he loved.

When Nancy exited the building, Cruz stretched his fingers in the leather gloves and pulled a black balaclava over his head so that only his eyes were visible.

The driver stepped out of the vehicle and opened the door. Nancy said something to her, and they both laughed. She slid into the back seat and her driver closed the door.

Cruz started across the parking lot, slowly at first so he wouldn't attract attention. When the driver climbed into the front seat, he accelerated. He drove from one lot to the next, fingers flexing on the steering wheel as he readied for the impact. The dark sedan had just pulled off when the bodyguard glanced over at Cruz gunning for them. Eyes wide in alarm, he threw up a hand and yelled something right before Cruz crashed the van into the car. Metal crushed metal and the airbags deployed.

The bodyguard couldn't get out because the van was wedged up against his dented door. Cruz grabbed the sledgehammer and hopped out of the van. He rushed around to the other side of the sedan and lifted a canister of pepper spray from a holster on his hip. He smashed the driver window. Glass scattered in the interior and all over the startled driver who cowered and lifted her hands in defense.

Cruz sprayed the interior with the noxious aerosol, waving his hand back and forth to get good coverage. The two in front hollered and Nancy covered her mouth and nose and grappled for the door to escape. Cruz set the hammer atop the car and yanked open the door, dragging her unceremoniously from the vehicle by the arm. Squinting, she made a valiant effort to fight by swinging on him, but he blocked the weak blow and then whipped the edge of his hand against the side of her neck, striking her carotid. She immediately went limp and he caught her with one hand before she fell to the pavement and then tossed her over his shoulder.

The driver tumbled from the sedan, face red, eyes running, and mucus dripping from her nose as she whimpered and clawed at her face for relief. Cruz ignored her and moved swiftly, collecting his tool and then going to the van. He placed Nancy on an old blanket he'd picked up at a thrift store and after she was settled, he slammed the door and climbed into the passenger seat. He backed away, watching as the bodyguard —tear-stained face contorted in agony—struggled with the broken door.

The entire smash and grab had taken less than sixty seconds.

Once he'd merged into traffic, Cruz whipped off the mask and turned down a side street. He drove for a couple of miles, making frequent turns, before heading down an alley to where he'd stashed an old blue Corolla. He hopped out of the van and checked the area before sliding open the back door.

Nancy was still unconscious, so he taped her mouth, legs, and hands behind her back. He opened the trunk of the blue car and placed her limp body inside a large bag and removed her wristlet, which contained keys and key cards—including one for the gym and the other for entry into her apartment building. Then he zipped up the bag.

Cruz tossed his weapons into the van, doused it in gasoline and tossed a match at the interior. The vehicle went up in flames.

He pulled out of the alley and drove to the next destination —Nancy's apartment.

_____

7

"You'll never get away with this."

Disheveled, with strands of black hair falling across her brow, Nancy stared at Cruz with angry eyes. But she could do nothing in her condition, shackled to the bars of the bed with butcher's twine he'd picked up at the supermarket.

"I've already gotten away with it."

Cruz had parked in front of her building and flung the bag with her inside over his shoulder. He used her key card to enter the building and took the stairs to the second floor. She awoke on the walk up. When her muffled whimpers and movement became excessive, he told her to shut up or he'd shoot her, and she simmered down.

"You could have talked to me," Nancy said.

"We both know you wouldn't have given me the information I wanted."

"What information do you want?"

"I told you I want to know where Shanice is."

"She's dead."

"She's not," Cruz said flatly.

"Well, if she's not, what makes you think I know anything about that?" She stared at him, giving nothing away.

"Because very few people have reason to keep her away from me."

She laughed, and her laughter grated on his nerves, turning his anger into acidic fury. "Sounds like wishful thinking to me. Maybe one of your enemies took her."

"You and I both know that's not true."

"I do not know that. It could have happened."

"It didn't."

"How do you know?"

He didn't have a lot of time to waste answering stupid questions. Soon, law enforcement would arrive at Nancy's place to start searching for clues to her disappearance.

Cruz removed a Beretta from its holster. Nancy's eyes followed his movement, but her face remained impassive.

He leaned forward, resting one hand on one knee. "No one has claimed credit. No one has asked for money or information or anything at all. I find that very odd, don't you?"

"Maybe they didn't know where to find you."

"Or maybe you took her because you thought you could change my mind about coming back to Plan B."

"Don't flatter yourself," Nancy spat.

"You had Miles calling me constantly after I left," Cruz reminded her.

"That's because you're a great asset, and I'd love for you to do another job, and Miles thought it would help take your mind off your girlfriend's death. But I certainly wouldn't kidnap your girlfriend to get you to come back."

"No?"

"No," she said firmly.

Cruz nodded, as if he'd accepted her answer. Then he removed a suppressor from his pocket and started screwing it on the end of the gun.

Nancy's eyes widened. "You can't seriously be thinking about killing me."

He shrugged. "You don't know anything. You're completely innocent and I've made a terrible mistake. I must get rid of the evidence now."

Nancy licked her lips. "W-wait a minute, Cruz. You're not thinking. If I do know something, then if you kill me, you'll lose any hope of finding Shanice."

"But you don't know anything," he reminded her.

"But what if I do?" she asked.

They stared at each other.

The anger inside him had bubbled up to blistering level. "Don't fuck with me, Nancy, I'm not in the mood. Tell me where she is, or I'll blow holes in your body and keep looking. We both know eventually I'll find her. Grabbing you was just an easier way, but I won't rest until I find her—with or without your help."

Nancy closed her eyes and sighed. She cursed softly and then looked at him again. "How do I know you won't kill me anyway?"

"The same way I don't know if you'll turn me in once I leave here. We both have to trust each other, and trust there will be no retaliation afterward."

In the silence, their eyes locked, and a nonverbal agreement was reached.

"She's alive."

Relief unexpectedly surged through Cruz. Until that moment, he hadn't fully processed the idea that Shanice was still alive. He'd been on auto-pilot. But now, receiving confirmation that she was truly among the living sent shock waves through his body and weakened him. He ran a hand down his face and swallowed hard.

"My goodness, you really love her, don't you?" Nancy looked

at him in wonder, like a scientist examining a newly found species of animal.

Cruz surged from the chair. Knee on the bed, he slammed the muzzle of the gun to Nancy's temple, none too gently. She let out a soft cry and turned away, but he continued shoving it against her skin, fighting the temptation to pull the trigger.

"And you let me think she was dead!" he snarled. "Give me one good reason not to kill you right now."

Shaking, Nancy answered, "Because I'll tell you where she is."

"Where is she?" he demanded.

"Promise me you won't kill me. I know you, Cruz. You're a man of your word. If you promise, you won't. Give me your word."

"Why should I? I know she's alive now."

"Because it'll be easier. Because you'll be reunited with her sooner."

The silence ticked slowly by. He had to control his emotions. He didn't want to be without Shanice one second longer than he had to.

"You have my word," Cruz said in a clipped tone. He removed himself from the bed.

Nancy let out a relieved breath through her mouth. "She's in Georgia, in a town outside of Atlanta—a place called Hopevale. We rented her a house. It's white—cute, but not in the best condition. It needed some work, but she liked it." Nancy shrugged. "I can't remember the exact street address, but it's on Rainbow Street, across from a brick ranch."

Cruz was confused by her description of the sequence of events. It all sounded so calm and orderly. "Doesn't sound like she was kidnapped," he said, which was what he'd thought. He'd thought she was somewhere out there, living in fear, perhaps knocked around by whomever was guarding her.

"We didn't kidnap her."

"Then how did you get her to leave me?" Cruz demanded.

Nancy averted her eyes. "While you were on the mission in Europe, we...we told her you were dead."

Unbelievable. They'd led them each to believe the other was dead.

"How did you figure out she was still alive?"

"Those lightweights you hired. Next time, get professionals."

"I thought we did, but apparently someone in the field cut corners." Nancy sounded annoyed, and he had the distinct impression that an employee was either getting fired or severely punished.

"Whose body was in my house? You blew up someone."

"We took a body from the morgue."

"You went through all that trouble to get me back? Why?" Cruz demanded.

Her face twitched with an emotion he couldn't define. "Because I had another job for you. Something important. I—"

A knock sounded at the front door, and they both froze.

Nancy arched an eyebrow. "What are you going to do?" she asked.

Cruz crossed to the window. Two police cars were parked outside. *Maldita.* They'd arrived sooner than he expected.

He scanned the room, and his gaze landed on the chair he'd abandoned. He locked the bedroom door and then took the chair over to the window.

He put the gun to Nancy's temple and she winced. "Don't ever come near Shanice again, do you hear me?"

"Yes," she replied from thinned lips.

"Can I count on you to keep your mouth shut about today?"

"Of course," she replied in the same tone.

Cruz brought his face down to hers. "If you don't, I'll be back."

They locked eyes.

"Hello?" a voice called uncertainly.

The officers had entered the apartment, probably with the assistance of the building superintendent.

"You'd better go."

Cruz re-holstered the weapon and using the chair as a battering ram, he slammed it into the window. The glass shattered and fell outside, a few pieces sprinkling inside onto the hardwood floor. He knocked off the remaining sharp edges as someone pounded on the door.

"Hey! Is someone here?" The doorknob wiggled.

"Help! Help!" Nancy called out. She'd had to do that, or she'd have to explain why she didn't when they finally made their way into the room.

Cruz tossed the chair aside and peered out the window at the almost thirty-foot drop.

"We're coming in!" Someone slammed into the door, splintering the frame, but the door didn't open.

Cruz climbed onto the window right as the door crashed open behind him from a second blow. He leaped into the air, landing soft-kneed on his feet and pushed into a forward roll.

"Hey! Stop!" someone yelled from the window.

He popped up and took off running. A piece of glass had cut through his shirt and nicked his arm, but he was otherwise unharmed.

Two shots were fired and he ducked his head, rounding the corner to where he'd parked the Corolla. He hopped in and pulled away. He'd have to ditch this vehicle immediately.

Next stop—Hopevale, Georgia.

8

P arked down the street, Cruz stared at the house. Like Nancy had said, the house was painted all white. It was late in the day and the sun had already gone down, leaving a stillness in the air—a quiet time as people gathered in their homes after a long day.

"Shanice," he murmured. His heart squeezed tight in his chest. His future was only blocks away.

He started the car and parked on the street outside the fence. Now that he was closer, he could see the work that needed to be done. Rotten wood around some of the windows needed to be replaced, and a fresh coat of paint would do wonders for the exterior—brighten it up a bit.

A woman with red hair was getting mail from her box and watched him get out of the vehicle. Cruz waved, and she waved back, a curious smile on her face.

He'd cut his hair, trimmed his beard, showered, and put on a clean white shirt, black pants, and shined his shoes for this visit. He hadn't seen Shanice in four months, not since he left on his last mission to Europe, and he wanted to look presentable.

He strolled up the stairs to the front door, but before he could ring the bell, the door was swung open and Shanice stood there with a phone to her ear.

"I placed the order a week ago, but they still haven't arrived..." Her mouth fell open when she saw him, and her hand with the phone slowly lowered in disbelief. "Cruz?" she whispered, looking like she'd seen a ghost.

"In the flesh, *mami*," he said, grinning.

Shanice wore a yellow shirt and matching yellow slacks. Her golden skin was glowing, and she wore her hair parted in the middle with the short curls framing her round face. Her brown eyes stared at him in wonder, her plump lips parted and painted an enticing pink color. She looked amazing.

Then her eyes rolled back in her head. *Oh damn.*

Cruz caught her before she collapsed at his feet. Lifting her into his arms, he took her inside and kicked the door shut. He placed her gently on the sofa and then went back to pick up her purse and phone, which had dropped from her hands.

Her fainting spell was short-lived. By the time he was on his knees at her side, she was waking up. Her eyes fluttered open and she stared at him in bewilderment.

"Is it really you, or am I dreaming?" she whispered.

"It's really me," he said.

She placed a hand to his face, touching his bearded cheek in wonder, as if she still didn't believe—needed further confirmation that he was, indeed, really there in her house. Her soft hands caressing his face were comforting but also stirred his blood.

He turned his face into her palm and placed a gentle kiss against her hand. Then he kissed her wrist and took a deep whiff of her honey and ginger scented skin. His favorite scent in the world.

Shanice sat up and swung her legs to the floor. Cruz joined her on the sofa.

"I don't understand. They—a woman named Nancy Cheng —she told me you were dead. She said she was the head of the Plan B organization. She showed me a picture of your body!" Her lower lip trembled.

"Clearly, it wasn't me. They made me believe you were dead, too."

Her eyes widened. "Why? What did they—she—have to gain?"

"She wanted me to return to Plan B and was willing to do anything to make that happen—including lie to us both."

"My god, that's awful." Then her face brightened, as if she'd just realized the magnitude of what had taken place. "You're here. You're alive."

"Yes." His face turned into a grin to match hers.

"You found me."

He nodded. "I found you. Once I guessed you were alive, I couldn't rest until I did."

Shanice flung herself into his arms and planted a kiss on his lips. Groaning, Cruz leaned back, pulling her on top of him. His fingers tunneled into her soft hair as he devoured her lips. His body hardened as his hands roamed over her hips and ass, getting familiar once more with her curves, his tongue tasting her delicious mouth, and nose filling with the sweetness of her scent.

There was nowhere else he'd rather be right now than with this woman. For four long months he hadn't been able to hold or kiss her. Now, finally, she was in his arms again.

Shanice closed her eyes and rested her forehead against his. "Please tell me you brought your clothes and everything else with you, because I'm not letting you out of my sight for a *very* long time."

Cruz chuckled, his hands cradling her ample bottom. "You'll be happy to know that I do have a few things with me, but eventually I'll need to get clothes and other items I had stored at the apartment in North Miami. You can come with me later when I get those. I didn't have much because to convince me that you were dead, they blew up my house and led me to believe you were in there. They even blew up a body they'd stolen from a morgue and claimed that was you through DNA analysis."

Her eyes widened. "Wow, they really went far."

"They did. They were very convincing."

"And you thought I was dead?" she said softly.

"I thought I'd lost you." His throat tightened, and his long fingers slipped into her curly hair. He kissed her. "Let me get my things from the car. I'll be right back."

"Okay." She didn't move from on top of him.

Cruz laughed. "You have to get up, sweetheart."

"I don't want to. I want to stay here with you and hold you forever." Sighing, she rested her head on his chest. "They told me you'd died. I can't stop thinking about that. I thought I'd never see you again, never hold you..." Her voice cracked.

"How did they convince you that I was dead? You said Nancy showed you pictures?"

Shanice nodded. "It was awful. I couldn't look at them. I only saw one. Maybe I should have known better, but...she was so convincing. She said you were murdered and the same people would come after me, so they needed to hide me. I packed my things and left your house. I was told I couldn't get in touch with any family or friends until they knew for sure I'd be safe. It could be *years*, she said. I took the name Mary Jones and settled here in Hopevale."

Cruz tightened his arms around her. "I'm sorry you had to go through that alone, but I'm here now."

She squeezed him back. "Promise me you won't leave me again," she whispered.

"I promise. My next job will be eight to five only."

She cupped his face and kissed him gently. "I got my baby

back. I love you."

"I love you, too."

CRUZ WENT OUT to the car and brought in his belongings. He left his bags by the door and joined Shanice in the kitchen where she was reheating leftover spaghetti and meatballs in the microwave. He stood in the doorway watching her as she moved around the kitchen, and a sense of peace and calm settled over him. He felt like he'd come home after a long, arduous journey.

That's what Shanice was for him. Home.

They ate at a small table in the kitchen, and he answered her questions about how he'd figured out she was alive and how he'd found her.

They finished the meal and washed the dishes, and then Cruz, with his back against the counter, pulled her into his arms.

"Thank you. I was starving."

"You're welcome, babe. I wish I had more. I know you have a big appetite." She nuzzled his neck.

"The only appetite I have right now is for you." Cruz slipped his hand under her shirt and caressed the soft skin of her back. "I've been trying to be good and patient, but I want you. I want you so damn much." He kissed her and she hummed her pleasure.

"Me, too. I want you so much."

"Let's go, before I lose my mind and fuck you right here on the floor."

She shivered in excitement, a naughty smile crossing her lips. "That's not such a bad idea."

He chuckled softly as she took his hand and led him out the kitchen.

9

In the bedroom, Shanice pressed her body against his. They were fully clothed, but she was already so aroused. Cruz was hard and solid, tall and broad, and he seemed to surround her with his presence. She'd been looking forward to this moment almost since she first saw him. Imagining what it would be like to loosen each of the buttons on his shirt and run her hands over his chest—to be in his arms and be made love to again.

He undressed her with great care, taking his time to pull the yellow shirt over her head and then helping her out of her pants by lowering to his haunches and tugging the material down her thighs. He kissed her inner thigh, his wet tongue stroking her skin in a slow, erotic glide of torture, while his big, rough-textured hands stroked down the back of her legs to her calves.

He removed her panties next and then he touched her *there*. His thumb caressed the slippery folds, and then he pressed his mouth into the dewy wet crease between her thighs. Shanice let out a helpless moan. The stubble on his face abraded her skin, adding another layer of sensation to his touch and making her knees weak. But she stood strong, grabbing onto his head as he took his time, gently touching her sensitive sex with his teeth and tongue.

Shanice's head fell back, and her body became as taut as a strained bowstring. "Cruz." She whispered his name to the ceiling, fingers tangled into the softness of his dark, silky hair.

But his goal wasn't to give her release right then, so he stood and made sure that she saw him lick the wetness from his lips, and she shivered a little at the carnal way he indulged in her taste.

He stripped bare in record time, tossing aside his clothes and shoes before pulling her on top of him on the bed. She could barely see him in the dark room yet eagerly examined him, pressing her lips to his strong throat and letting her hands roam freely over the muscles of his chest and tight abs. The man was magnificent, a machine, a warrior—in the truest sense of the word.

Shanice lowered her head and kissed him. Their lips glided over each other, and she teased him with her tongue, forcing his to chase hers, withdrawing each time they touched. He finally grabbed the back of her head, and their tongues tangled together in a sexy, snakelike dance.

Then he took his time, tasting her skin and gently sucking on the base of her throat. Straddling his torso, she rubbed her aching clit against him, until Cruz uttered a soft curse and flipped them over.

She watched his head go lower as he kissed between her aching breasts. Her nipples tightened as his hands skimmed her torso, his slow, torturous movements heightening her anticipation. Shanice ran her fingers roughly through his wavy hair and over his broad shoulders. He was taking his time, and she wanted to scream—unclear in her own mind if she needed him to stop or hurry up.

He sucked the engorged nipple of her left breast into his mouth, and it throbbed to painful life. His tongue flicked over and around it, savoring the caramel tip in a leisurely way as if he had hours available to enjoy himself. Then he gave her breast a long lick from the bottom to the top. Shanice shivered and tightened her grip on his head. While his mouth kept that breast busy, his hand became preoccupied with the right one. She arched back and twisted, an insistent throbbing echoing between her thighs like a second heartbeat.

When he finished with her breasts, Cruz went lower and caressed her thighs and calves with his hands and mouth. She became lost in the feelings he created, lost in the touch of his hands and his expert, enticing kisses. Moaning, she didn't know how much more torture she could take. By the time he came back up to her mouth, she thought she was going a little bit crazy.

Sliding a hand into his hair, she pulled him closer and tighter on top of her body.

"I want you. *Please*," she begged. They'd been apart for months and she needed him so much, she was like a giant livewire.

Shanice angled her pelvis higher to drive home the point, and Cruz chuckled against her collarbone, his warm breath brushing her skin like a light feather.

"Why you so anxious, *mami*?" he teased.

"You arrogant..."

Eyes filled with humor, he kissed her hard and wrapped her legs around him, centered the hard ridge of his dick between her legs. She throbbed, ached, and was consumed by fire. The greedy, devouring kiss only deepened the need to be taken by him. But she resigned herself to prolonging their lovemaking, showing him how much she adored him by touching everywhere her hands could reach.

Over and over they explored each other as if it were the first time. She kissed his back, where scars marred his smooth skin. She kissed his thighs, the hairs that were sprinkled on his skin tickling her lips. And then she sucked his balls and licked the veined underside of the rigid column of flesh at the apex of his thighs, smiling to herself as she listened to him swear softly at the same time a shudder of pleasure rocked his frame.

Cruz hauled her back up to the pillows and pressed her into the mattress. His heavy-lidded eyes were filled with deep, dark hunger. "*Ahora*," he said with determination. *Now*.

His hands coasted down her sides and over her hips, and she whimpered softly, breath coming faster in expectation. Then he lifted her hips and slid his thick shaft into her waiting wetness.

Inch by torturous inch, Cruz slid deeper, nostrils flaring and a throaty groan coming from deep in his chest. It was so sexy, so empowering to hear him enjoy being inside her so much.

Shanice shifted, determined to take all of him. She arched her hips higher, signaling her readiness, and he thrust all the way in, seated to the hilt. She gasped, and her eyes drifted closed, fingernails digging into his tight backside and eliciting a gasp from him.

"You still belong to me, *mami*?" he asked huskily. His teeth nipped at her earlobe.

"Yes," she moaned.

In every sense of the word, she was his. She blinked back the tears of emotion that pricked her eyes.

Cruz moved, his rough, pounding strokes jiggling her breasts, while Shanice eagerly met each downward thrust with the upswing of her hips. He felt so good, all she could do was moan and whimper. Their raw, powerful passion flared out of control as Shanice cried out—the sound partly from the exquisite sensation of his possession, but also from the emotion of their bodies coming together again after so long.

Each stroke was deep and hard, breath-stealing, mind-blowing. She clutched his shoulders, clawed his sides, and gripped his butt. Her hands were everywhere, sliding over satin-covered muscle and encouraging him to keep going—to take her over the brink to ecstasy.

Cruz pushed her legs up and open, limiting her movements and taking total control. She lost count of how many times his hips pumped against hers. She only knew that the pleasure was never-ending.

Cruz smacked her ass, and she reveled in the sting of his hand. He hit her again, and her broken, choked cry filled the room as his hand connected with her tender ass cheek.

"You know I love this ass," he muttered with a gleam in his eyes.

She was close to climaxing, and when Cruz hit her again, one hand gripped the sheets and the other fastened around his thick neck. Her mouth fell open and a ragged cry tore from the depths of her throat.

Orgasmic waves rippled through her body. She trembled and gasped as she convulsed. Right after, Cruz went rigid. She barely heard him as he whispered in Spanish, but she did catch the words *mi vida*—my life.

He collapsed beside her, and they both lay on their backs, staring up at the ceiling. Once her breathing was almost back to normal, Shanice scooted over and nestled close to him. She kissed his shoulder and then he turned on his side and flung an arm across her waist. Neither said a word. They just closed their eyes, faces close together, bodies centimeters apart.

Later, after they'd rested, he caressed her body, seducing her with his touch, and she willingly melted in his arms again. The first time was slower, a sensual reacquaintance after time apart. The second time was rougher, more carnal, more out of control.

With a firm hand on her back, Cruz pushed Shanice into

the mattress and claimed her body with savage strokes—his pelvis crashing against her bottom until she was gasping and gripping the sheets, her moans and eventual cries of ecstasy stifled in the pillows.

10

Cruz couldn't stop staring at Shanice. *She's alive.*

Nothing else mattered. He didn't care about the physical possessions he'd lost in the explosion, which were all replaceable. Shanice was alive.

They were both lying on their sides, facing each other, and he had an arm placed loosely across her waist. Her eyes were closed, and the colorful sheet was wrapped around her thick body but dipped low enough to offer a glimpse at the fullness of her breasts and the rounded caramel tops of her areolas. He knew his woman's body, and her breasts were fuller and oddly, her areolas were darker—or so it seemed. Maybe his mind was playing tricks on him.

Her hair was a sexy, rumpled mess, her lips plumped from his ardent kisses, and even in sleep, her cheeks maintained a faint flush from their lovemaking. She mumbled something and changed position. Cruz smoothed a hand over her hair and she settled down, her breathing returning to an even in-and-out sound. He looked at her for a few minutes longer, still in disbelief that he'd found her alive and well.

Finally, the call of hunger in his stomach could no longer be ignored, and he eased off the bed, careful not to disturb her. The photo on the nightstand made him smile. He knew how much she'd enjoyed that particular night they went dancing, and he was glad she was able to take the picture from the house.

He tugged on his boxer briefs and quietly left the room. Outside in the hallway, he realized that he'd been so happy about their reunion that he hadn't taken a tour of the house.

Shanice had told him there were four bedrooms upstairs. He opened the room next to the master and peered in. There weren't any curtains or blinds on the windows, so the light pouring into the room came from the streetlights out front.

He frowned as he examined the décor. Was he seeing right?

Cruz flipped on the light. A paint can and brushes were in one corner atop a folded painter's drop cloth. Yellow paint covered three walls, and on one of the walls he saw dinosaurs and other stickers.

What the...?

His heartrate accelerated. Was this room what he thought it was? Was this a *baby room*?

Running his fingers through his hair, Cruz stepped farther across the carpeted floor, unable to take his eyes from the wall.

Shanice was pregnant. She had to be. There was no other explanation for why she'd decorate one of the bedrooms in such a fashion. She was having his baby, and that explained the differences he noticed in her body.

Cruz ran a hand down his face. Becoming a parent was not in his immediate plans, but he was not turned off by the idea at all. He planned to live a different life now with the woman he loved. He'd thought about marrying her and was startled but excited by the prospect of becoming a father.

But why hadn't she said anything to him?

Cruz mulled that question while he visited the two bathrooms and last two bedrooms. Then he took the stairs to the first floor and walked through the downstairs part of the house, getting acquainted with its sounds and silences. That way, if there was the slightest shift in temperature or he experienced that intangible sensation that crept to the back of his neck, he'd notice—letting him know there was an intruder or someone had been inside the house.

In the kitchen, he poured himself some orange juice and made a meal with food he found in the refrigerator. The spaghetti had been good but he was hungry again. He made toast, scrambled four eggs, and fried several pieces of ham. Then he sat at the table in the breakfast nook and consumed half the meal in record time.

Shanice entered the kitchen, wrapped in a pale pink robe, her cheeks rosy, hair combed into some semblance of order, and her eyes bright and shiny. She looked happy, like a woman who'd been thoroughly made love to by the man she loved.

"Hey, there," she said, going over to the refrigerator.

"Hey." Cruz continued eating, slower this time as he watched her move around the kitchen.

"When do you want to go pick up the rest of your stuff from Miami?"

"I'm in no rush. Anything that I absolutely need, I can buy for now."

She sat down across from him with a glass of water. "Good. Then we can spend a couple of days exploring Hopevale. I'm still getting used to it myself, but it'll be fun to take a tour and get to know the town and all its hidden places together." Her face beamed across the table at him.

"I agree. By the way, I took a tour of the house while you were sleeping. Saw all the bedrooms. Anything you want to tell me?" Cruz set down his fork and gave her his undivided attention.

"Oh." The smile died on her face, and she gazed into her glass of water.

Cruz suddenly had a sobering thought. What if she hadn't mentioned the baby because he wasn't the father? A piece of ham caught in his throat, and he swallowed it past the burning in his chest. Was it possible that maybe she'd quickly moved on after she thought he was dead? Perhaps seeking solace in another man's arms, and gotten pregnant?

"Is the baby mine?" he asked.

Her eyes flew up to his, her brow creasing. "Yes, the baby is yours."

Although relieved by her answer, he asked, "Then why didn't you tell me?"

"It didn't exactly come up in conversation, Cruz. We talked and then...and then we made love. Baby talk wasn't a priority at the time." Agitated, she stood with her glass and went over to the sink. She stared out the window at the back yard.

Cruz followed her. "What's going on, Shanice? Is there something you're not telling me?" He examined her profile, looking for clues to her emotional state.

Taking a deep breath, she turned to face him. "I guess I wasn't sure."

"You weren't sure about what?" Cruz asked.

"About you."

"Me?"

Maybe she was hesitant about his ability to be a good father. During their time together, he'd shared information about his past. About how his father hadn't been dependable, and about how he'd eventually abandoned Cruz and his mother for a life abroad.

Herberto Cordoba had found his calling as an entrepreneur in Cuba. He had quite a few businesses, including selling time on multiple Internet accounts and traveling to Europe and bringing back household items and electronics to sell on the black market. During one of his trips to Europe, he promised to send for Cruz and his mother, said they'd have a family vacation. Cruz vividly remembered the day his father left. Their last hug, the kiss he'd given his mother. But Herberto had never sent for them—breaking yet another one of many promises he'd made over the years.

When Cruz's mother fell ill and eventually passed, he was certain his father would do the right thing, but instead, Cruz was forced to live in a tiny apartment with his grandmother and her two sisters. He found out years later that his father had died, too, about five years after his mother's passing.

His grandmother's home was loving, but they had very little. Anger had simmered inside him for a long time because of the neglect of his father and the loss of both parents at a young age. That volatile emotion had steered him in the wrong direction too many times. He'd used his brute strength and pent-up anger to pummel his way into a life of crime, which had luckily been short-lived thanks to Plan B. Were it not for the organization channeling his energy, seeing a better use for his bright mind and fighting ability, who knew where he'd be today. Probably dead or in prison.

"Yes, I wasn't sure about you. Cruz, let's be honest here. We fell for each other very fast. Within a very short time I had moved in with you, and then you were gone. Then we both thought we were dead! We haven't been in a long-term relationship, and to toss a baby into the mix..." She shrugged, uncertainty in her eyes.

He was relieved. Her hesitation was not for the reason he thought. "You want this baby, right?"

"Yes."

"I want this baby, too. I'm looking forward to being a father."

Cruz intended to be the complete opposite of the example of fatherhood he'd received from Herberto. His father had never kept his promises, and he wanted to be the type of father he'd never had. Affectionate. Present. A keeper of promises.

Her tight shoulders deflated with relief. "Really?" she asked.

"Really."

"You're sure?"

"Yes. Very sure." He smiled at her.

Her face brightened again, her sensual lips curving upward at the corners. "Okay."

"Anything else?" Cruz took her hand.

"Well, there is one more thing. I want to stay in Hopevale. I've only been here a little while, but it reminds me a lot of where I grew up in Texas. I know the neighbors, and I've gotten to know a few of the shopkeepers on Main Street. It's the perfect size town—not too big, not too small. Before, I was worried about revealing too much because I had to hide my past and who I was, but now I can really be a part of this community and raise our child here." Anxiety crept back into her eyes.

"Did you forget my home was in Islamorada? I'll miss being near the water, but if you're here, I like it, too. And when I want excitement, Atlanta is only thirty-five minutes away, right?"

She stepped into him and wrapped her arms around his waist. "So, you think you could live here?"

"As long as I'm with you, I can live anywhere."

Her eyes softened, and she rose onto her toes. "You're going to make me love you even more," she whispered against his lips.

"*Bueno*. My plan is working."

Then he took her mouth in a soft kiss.

11

S hanice hung up the phone and entered the last bedroom at the end of the hall where Cruz was painting. "Your conversation with the landlord worked. A rep from the company is coming first thing in the morning to fix the garage door."

Cruz had heard the frustration in her voice when she was talking to the landlord earlier, and after she ended the call, he'd asked her what was wrong. She explained about the garage, and when he found out how long the door had been broken, he'd been furious. He demanded the phone and redialed the number.

"It's handled," he'd said, after getting off the phone.

She wasn't sure the landlord would follow through after being such a jerk for weeks, but unfortunately, some men only responded to other men. He called back a few minutes ago to let her know he'd set the appointment.

"If they don't show up tomorrow, I'll pay him a visit," Cruz said, dipping the rolling brush in the pan of paint.

Two weeks had passed by in a flurry of do-it-yourself projects. They were painting the last bedroom, or rather, Cruz was painting. Shanice had chosen a light tan color—sugar cookie, according to the color wheel from the paint store.

He was bare-chested, his broad back on display, muscles rippling when he moved, and the jeans fitting nice and snug on his fantastic ass. She ogled him as he smoothed the rolling brush down the wall. Then, unable to resist any longer, she went over and wrapped her arms around his waist from behind.

"I'm working," he said, amusement in his voice.

"And doing a great job, I might add." She rubbed a palm over the muscles and scars on his back. She wished she could make the marks disappear, as well as the two torturous days during which they'd been inflicted.

One night Cruz had told her the story of how he'd gotten the scars. He'd been on a mission where they'd received bad intel. They'd been outnumbered and ambushed, and Cruz was tied to a wooden pole and tortured by having a sharp blade dragged across his back. He'd been one of the few to eventually escape, but the scars remained as a harsh reminder of what had occurred.

He paused. "You like the color, right?"

Shanice sighed exaggeratedly. "I changed my mind *one* time."

"After I had already painted half the room," he grumbled.

"Be glad it wasn't the whole room."

He glanced over his shoulder and she smiled sweetly. Cruz narrowed his eyes at her.

"When did your mother say she was coming?" Cruz asked, setting down the brush.

"She hasn't decided yet, but she's looking at flights around November. I'll be pretty far along by then. How are things going with your plans?" she asked.

In between working on the house, he'd been looking

around for a location for his security firm, though he hadn't done much work on that because of the home repairs.

"After I finish up here, I'll get on the computer and find a real estate agent. Looking on my own hasn't turned up much."

"What type of location are you looking for? You never told me if you wanted to build or buy something already built."

"Because I hadn't decided, but after some thought, if I could find a suitable building, that would be better. Less expensive, and I could open the business faster. We'll need a place big enough to provide temporary housing, like a dorm-style setup for new trainees. A kitchen, a firing range or a place for one so staff can practice and stay sharp. I'll need a communications room, office space, et cetera, et cetera. I won't bore you with the details, but some level of privacy would be necessary, too."

"You don't want much," Shanice quipped.

"No," he said with a laugh. "But if I'm going to do this, I'm going to do it right and big—at least here. Eventually, I want to have offices in other locations around the country—but this will be our headquarters and where I want training to take place. And, since the Atlanta airport is the busiest in the world, setting up in Hopevale is not such a bad idea."

"Aren't you glad I convinced you to stay?"

"Yes, thank you." He gave her a quick kiss and stepped back to look at the painting he'd completed. "Almost done."

"You know, there might be a place for you to buy."

Cruz lifted an eyebrow in inquiry.

"Mr. Garner was complaining about an abandoned property a while back." Mr. Garner was in his sixties and their regular mail carrier. He was a good source of information to learn the history of Hopevale, as well as finding out the latest gossip about various residents. "The property is fifteen miles from here and used to be a church compound, but after a scandal where it was discovered that the pastor fathered two kids outside of his marriage, the ministry fell apart and the property went into foreclosure. No one's bought it yet."

"How long ago was this?" Cruz asked, definitely looking interested.

"Let's see, I think Mr. Garner said it's been five years since the ministry shut down. We could look it up. Water of Life Ministries was the name. He did say the grounds are overrun with weeds, but the buildings might still be in good shape and can be renovated."

"Hmm. Fifteen miles from here?"

Shanice nodded. "About that."

"Let's take a break and check it out."

CRUZ STOOD outside the chain-link fence with Shanice, overlooking the property from the highway. Like the mail carrier had said, the place was overrun with weeds and bushes, but all the buildings were still standing, and most of them were made of solid brick. Their online research uncovered that the Water of Life Ministries main building used to contain class-rooms in the basement, a fellowship hall with a kitchen, and elsewhere on the property, a halfway house for recovering addicts. There was an outdoor pavilion for taking advantage of warm summer days and a gymnasium where members could play basketball. The property was visible from the highway with a road leading into the large parking lot, but the back side butted up against a boundary of trees.

Shanice gripped the fence. "What do you think?"

"I can definitely see the possibilities. Hell, I think it's perfect. This might be the place."

"Yeah?" Her eyes brightened with excitement. Knowing she was just as excited as he was made him smile.

"Yeah." He grabbed her around the waist, and she squealed with happiness, winding her arms around his neck.

He was about to give her an appreciative kiss when the phone rang. Miles.

Cruz hadn't heard from him in a while. The last time they'd talked, Cruz had called and told him that he'd found Shanice alive.

"Hello?"

"Hey, Cruz. Got a minute?" His voice sounded oddly strained.

Cruz was instantly on the alert. "Sure."

"You alone?"

"I'm with Shanice. We're looking at a property that might become the headquarters for my new security firm." When she tossed a curious expression his way, he mouthed Miles's name. Then he walked several feet away to continue the conversation in private. "What's going on, Miles? You don't sound too good."

"I know you haven't heard because you're no longer tuned in, but things are a mess here in DC. Nancy is dead."

Startled, Cruz froze. "Cheng?"

"Yes. She didn't come back from lunch yesterday. Her assistant said she had a meeting that wasn't on her calendar. They found her body in her car near Deanwood Station."

Cruz knew the Deanwood area. It was one of the oldest in Northeast DC with a rich history, including being the boyhood home of Marvin Gaye, but the high crime rate was a stain on the community. What had Nancy been doing in that part of town?

"How did she die?" he asked.

"Looks like suicide. Bullet wound under the chin and gunshot residue on her hands. She shot herself."

Cruz's mind whirled in disbelief.

"Did you do it?"

Cruz turned away from Shanice. "Hell, no. And you just said it was suicide."

"I said it *looks* like suicide. I don't know what the hell is going on, but I don't believe for one minute that Nancy killed herself. Do you?"

"No, and she wouldn't have to drive to another part of DC to take her own life, but that doesn't mean I did it."

"Sorry, I had to ask. I can't exactly forget how angry you were when you left my house when we figured out Nancy had to be the person responsible for Shanice's disappearance. Then you find out where Shanice is, right after Nancy was kidnapped, coincidentally. Snatching her like that had you written all over it, but Nancy provided little help to the investigators, and they never found the culprit."

Cruz didn't bother to deny he was the one who'd taken Nancy. There was no reason to because they both knew he'd done it. "If Nancy didn't kill herself, someone killed her. But why?"

"The million-dollar question." Miles sounded tired, as if he'd spent a lot of time studying the angles of Nancy's death and came up empty-handed.

"There's something going on that we're not aware of, and I have to wonder if it involves me."

"What makes you say that?" Miles asked.

"Something she said to me when I talked to her last. She said she had an important job for me, that's why she'd asked you to get in touch, but she never told me what it was. It was the *way* she said it, as if there was an extra meaning behind the words. That conversation has been at the back of my mind ever since."

"Could mean anything. Could mean nothing."

"Maybe." But Cruz trusted his instincts.

Cars whizzed by on the highway behind him, and he

glanced at Shanice, who was leaning against the car, head bent as she texted on her phone.

He turned away again. "Who's investigating?" he asked.

"No one. Right now, they're treating her death like a suicide."

"Was there a note?"

"No."

Cruz frowned, thinking. "She was silenced for a reason."

"But why and by who?" Miles sounded frustrated.

Cruz could imagine him pacing his office. "Who's going to take over the director position?"

"They're still deciding, but I'm under consideration."

"Do you want it?"

"Yes and no. Hell, Plan B is the reason I no longer have a wife. I'm not so sure getting deeper into the organization is a good idea, but we do good work—thankless work because very few people know who we are or what we do, but I'm proud of that work."

Cruz nodded. "I give you a hard time, but you deserve the position, Miles. I hope you get it—if that's what you want."

"Yeah, well, we'll see. A decision hasn't been made yet, and I'm not sure I want to be director, dealing with politicians and answering ridiculous questions about our missions. I'd rather stay down here in the belly of the beast and get the work done. But...well, we'll see. Listen, I've gotta run. Go back to spending time with your woman and looking at office space. Sounds like you're assimilating into civilian life pretty easily."

"Yeah." He wasn't so sure.

He'd stayed busy working on the house with Shanice, but every now and again a restlessness overcame him. He missed the adrenalin rush of the clandestine assignments he used to perform. Giving up that life was like quitting a drug cold-turkey, and he probably would have been better off getting slowly weaned off the stimulant.

"Enjoy it. Good luck to you and your new life."

"Thanks. Hey, do me a favor." Cruz cast a glance at Shanice again. For a minute, his heart constricted and he hesitated. He didn't want to get involved. He had her and their unborn child to think about. Nonetheless, call it curiosity or simply habit, he felt himself getting sucked in. "Keep me in the loop."

"I thought you were done with Plan B," Miles said.

"I am, but...keep me in the loop. Let me know if you find out anything else. I'm not happy about what Cheng did, keeping me and Shanice apart, but if she was murdered, I'd like to know why."

"I'll let you know what I find out, if anything. But this was professional, Cruz. A clean kill. The kind of thing you or one of our other agents would do. I don't think we'll know who killed her anytime soon. Maybe never."

With those last words, Miles hung up.

Cruz tapped the phone against his palm. Nancy Cheng's death was none of his business. He'd stay out of it and only get his information from Miles. He'd told Shanice he was leaving his dangerous work behind, and he intended to keep his word.

He walked back over to where she was standing.

"Everything okay?" she asked, fixing curious eyes on him.

"Everything's fine," Cruz answered.

12

Cruz looped an arm around Shanice's throat from behind and brushed his nose along her neck, making her skin tingle. "You smell good," he said.

He was taking her out to a nice dinner and referred to the evening as a belated birthday celebration since he missed the big day a couple of months ago, and he hadn't been pleased to learn she hadn't done anything special.

She straightened her clothes, eyeing her reflection in the bathroom mirror. The long-sleeved dress embraced her curves and her now obvious pregnant belly with clingy cotton. The colorful material highlighted her hips, and the dipping neckline showed off her ample bosom and the gold necklace with a heart-shaped pendant resting on her cleavage. Cruz had given her the jewelry moments before, part of the evening's events, which included dinner at a steak restaurant that promised the best steaks in the south. Being from Texas, she knew good beef and looked forward to finding out just how hyperbolic their advertising was.

She turned her head and kissed his smooth jaw. He'd

shaved a while back, getting rid of the stubble she'd come to enjoy scraping along her skin. "You do, too."

His cologne filled her nostrils, an intoxicating blend of citrus and sandalwood.

"And you look nice," she added, smoothing a hand down the front of his long-sleeved white shirt. He'd paired it with a black tie and black slacks.

"Thank you. You almost ready, *mami*?" he asked, patting her bottom before walking away.

"Almost."

Shanice applied glossy coral color to her mouth and pressed her lips together. Tonight reminded her of their first date when he took her to La Cocina Patagonia on South Beach. Their meal had been delicious, and the kiss at her front door had fanned the flames of her desire for him, confirming their chemistry in no uncertain terms. She'd been nervous and excited then and deeply attracted to him. Tonight, she wasn't nervous but anxiously looked forward to their date since most of their outings had been lowkey so far, and their days filled with routine tasks like grocery-shopping, cooking meals together, and washing the cars in the driveway.

In Islamorada, they'd gone out once a week, but of course, that had been a different time. They'd been through a traumatic experience—new for her—and those weeks had been special, a way to bond and learn more about each other and enjoy each other's presence. She wanted more of that, without the encumbrances of worrying about the future, work, and fixing up this house.

Two months in, and they were done with the repairs. The painting was completed, the hardwood floors redone by professionals, the rotted wood on the outside replaced, and the landlord had fixed the garage and painted the exterior of the house.

Despite all the positive developments, there was an issue

that Shanice hadn't mentioned but stayed at the back of her mind.

Marriage.

They were having a baby, but Cruz hadn't broached the subject of getting married since he learned she was pregnant, and she hadn't, either. Was he one of those people who didn't need to be married to raise a family together? She wished she could be one of the modern women who didn't care about a ring, but in all honesty, she wanted one. She wanted the life she'd seen her parents share, and at some point, she and Cruz would have to discuss their plans for the future. For now, she'd continue to revel in the fact that she had her man back and their easy-going, fun-loving relationship. She didn't want to cause friction between them—yet.

Turning sideways, Shanice eyed her bump—evidence of the life growing inside of her. She placed a hand on her prominent belly. At least she'd soon have her mother by her side, guiding her during the last months of the pregnancy and available to help after the birth.

They left the house and Cruz drove to the restaurant in the dining district, an area filled with the options of all types of cuisines—from vegan to steak, Mexican to Italian—whatever you wanted in fine dining, there was an establishment serving dishes to satisfy those cravings.

Their restaurant was located with nine others in an abandoned high school building. Cruz parked at the front, and a valet opened Shanice's door.

"Thank you," she murmured, looking up at the exterior.

Cruz took her hand as they walked to the double doors, and she leaned into him, absorbing the physical contact and the power emanating from him. At times she wondered if touching could be even more important to him than it was to her. She was used to hugging, kissing, and showing affection to family members. He'd been starved of those normalities for years in his line of work.

"I hope the food is good." He planted a gentle kiss on her temple.

They entered side by side and walked down the hallway, which remained pretty much unchanged from the days children and teachers roamed the halls. They walked along the tiled floor to a door on the right, where a gold plate on the wall announced the Chattahoochee River Steak House. Cruz gave his name, and they were escorted to a small table near the back. He sat facing the door, and Shanice settled across from him, her appetite spiking as the scent of the fragrant food wafted into her nostrils.

They ordered their meals—a T-bone for Shanice and grilled trout and a sirloin for Cruz. Shanice sipped sweet tea and Cruz sipped wine in the quiet ambiance, eyes lingering on each other.

"What are you thinking about?" Cruz asked.

"Remembering our first date, when you took me to La Cocina Patagonia. Seems like a lifetime ago."

"But it was only what...six, seven months ago?"

She sighed heavily. "I know. I can't believe it."

He reached across the table and took one of her hands in his. "Tonight, I don't want you to think about anything negative. Tonight we'll pretend it's your birthday, which I should have been able to share with you. Okay?"

"Okay."

"Good. By the way, I talked to Raheem earlier and he wants to come for a visit in November and stay for a couple of weeks. He said I've gone soft by entering civilian life and settling down."

"Tell him not everyone wants to chase ass all their lives. Matter of fact, I can tell him myself when he arrives." Cruz and

Raheem talked often, and she liked Raheem and couldn't wait to see him.

Cruz laughed softly. Gosh, when he smiled, it transformed his face.

"I'll pass on the message."

"You like where we live, right?" Shanice asked.

Although she believed he appreciated their mellow lifestyle in Hopevale, she needed confirmation. Sometimes she wondered if he missed going on missions, but didn't dare ask, in case the answer was yes. Selfishly, she wanted him to herself and couldn't stand the thought of him constantly putting himself in harm's way. Though the photos Nancy Cheng had shown her were fake, that didn't mean someone couldn't hurt Cruz like that one day. He wasn't invincible.

"Of course. I'm looking forward to years of quiet."

"Good." Shanice relaxed. "My mother will be here soon, so we'll have a couple of guests, and it'll be nice to see Raheem again."

"I think he wants to get away for a while, anyway," Cruz remarked.

"What's his story?" she asked. "How did he end up working for Plan B?" Raheem was like Cruz. He didn't have much of a family.

Cruz paused before launching into his friend's background. "When he was eight, his father disappeared. Left for work and never came back. He left him and his younger brother with his mother, an abusive piece of shit, from the stories he's told me. She got a kick out of knocking Raheem and his brother around. When he was about twelve, his brother got run over and died—a tragic accident. The beatings became worse because Raheem's mother blamed him, said he should have been looking out for his brother.

"He finally ran away from home when he was fifteen, lived on people's couches, but he had a skill with computers, so he could fix them and set up in-home networks, things like that, for the people he stayed with. He got a part-time job at a local computer repair shop after school and caught Plan B's attention when he was sixteen. Upset that the CEO of a poorly-performing company was getting a bonus, he hacked into the corporation's mainframe and direct deposited checks to all the employees who were losing their jobs."

"Quite an accomplishment for a teenager."

Cruz agreed with a nod.

Shanice had always known she was fortunate to grow up in a stable home environment, and though her father died long before she'd expected him to, she'd been lucky to have two loving parents and a loud, extended family.

She spent Christmas surrounded by the sounds of carols, the scent of baking cookies, and the laughter of family who came by to visit. Cruz, Raheem, and the others like them in the agency never had that, and she suddenly desperately wanted to create that atmosphere so they'd have new, happy memories to replace old, damaging ones.

"When he gets here, I want to offer him a job at the Cordoba Agency," Cruz said, referring to the name he'd chosen for his security firm.

"I think that's a great idea. I hope he accepts."

"I hope so, too. I guess I'll have to make the offer enticing enough so he will."

They finished eating their meal, and at the end of dinner, the waiter arrived and collected their empty plates. He was in his thirties, with curly hair and a winsome smile. "How was everything?" he asked.

"My meal was excellent," Cruz responded.

The waiter turned his attention to Shanice. "And your steak?"

Cruz arched an eyebrow at her.

"Very good," she replied, with a smile.

"That's what we like to hear. Can I interest either of you in dessert?"

"Apple pie with ice cream for me," Shanice said.

"I'll have a slice of cake. Could you remind me of your options?"

The waiter leaned across the table and said in a conspiratorial voice, "You know, we have a delicious red velvet cake that's off-menu. Would you like to try that?" His gaze shifted between them.

Shanice's eyes widened. "Red velvet? That's my favorite. Now I have to decide..." She pouted.

"Get them both. I would," Cruz said.

"Well, this *is* a night of celebration." She bit the corner of her lip. "And since I'm eating for two..."

Cruz chuckled, eyes filled with indulgent humor because she'd used the "eating for two" excuse plenty of times.

"I don't want to, but okay, I'll take both. If I can't eat it all, I'll take one of them home."

"Or I'll eat what you don't want."

"No," Shanice said firmly. He consumed so many calories in a day, at times she wondered if he had a bottomless pit as a stomach. "I'll eat my own dessert, thank you."

As Cruz laughed, the waiter clasped his hands together, a smile of amusement on his face at their little disagreement. "Sounds good. I'll be right back."

When he'd disappeared, Cruz asked, "I'm glad to hear you enjoyed the steak."

"I've had better, but I didn't want to be catty. It was good enough."

"Good enough? I'm glad you didn't say that to the waiter. He might have tossed us out of here. This is, after all, where they grill the best steaks in the south."

Resting her chin on her hand, Shanice shook her head at

him. "You have a snarky sense of humor, Mr. Cordoba. I hope our baby has my temperament."

"I'm not so sure about that. I think we'll be better off if he's more like me than you."

They spent the next few minutes teasing each other about whose personality their child would be better off having. Shanice was so distracted she didn't notice the waiter returning until he was next to the table, along with six other servers.

"Shanice, we were told that you're celebrating your birthday today," he announced, placing her pie on the table, followed by an eight-inch round buttercream cake with an unlit candle in the center.

Shanice's mouth fell open. With his thick arms folded on the table, Cruz's dark eyes sparkled at her. This cake had *not* been made at the restaurant. He had clearly remembered that red velvet was her favorite and arranged for the cake to be here and brought out.

The waiter lit the sole candle and then moved into a huddle with his co-workers. "One, two—one, two, three...Happy birthday to you..."

Cruz and the seven servers serenaded Shanice with the happy birthday song while she rocked side to side in the chair, enjoying the attention. She couldn't stop grinning. Tonight was the complete opposite of the depressing way she'd spent her actual birthday—missing Cruz, wishing her life were different. Little did she know that in mere weeks, he'd be back in her life and happiness would become the norm.

When the singing finished, Shanice blew out the candle and the staff and a few people at the surrounding tables clapped.

Thank you, Shanice mouthed to Cruz, as one of the female servers handed plates and a knife to their waiter.

You're welcome, he mouthed, his love for her evident in his eyes.

Soon, they each had a piece of red velvet cake in front of them, and she slid the moist dessert off the fork and into her mouth. "Mmm. Did you get this from the bakery on Main Street?"

Cruz shook his head. "Aunt Bessie's Sweets N Things, one street over, right here in the dining district."

"I've never been to that bakery. I need to check them out." Shanice set down her fork. Gazing across at Cruz, she hoped he saw how much she loved him and how much she appreciated what he'd done for her tonight. Her big, tough man was also a softie—sweet and romantic. "Thank you again, babe."

"It wasn't much, but I wanted you to have a little celebration and enjoy yourself."

His eyes smiled across the table at her, and Shanice melted inside.

"I did." She blew Cruz a kiss and then tucked into her dessert.

13

After dinner, they strolled hand-in-hand down the street in the cool autumn air and checked out some of the other restaurants in the dining district, making plans to visit them before circling back to get the car for the ride to a small music venue.

Cruz had asked around for a good place to listen to music, and the lounge he ended up choosing was small, with exposed brick walls and a cozy, intimate vibe. Shanice relaxed in the crook of his arm as the talented musicians and their female lead singer beguiled the crowd with a mix of jazz and neo soul.

After an hour, Cruz and Shanice had decided to leave when Cruz heard raucous male laughter above the relaxing music.

"Come on, sweetheart, don't be so stuck up," a man's deep voice said.

More boisterous laughter.

Cruz glanced to his left. A big guy with meaty hands and a gut that rivaled Santa Claus had their waitress, Jemma, by the wrist. The man's friends were grinning like the tools they were, encouraging his behavior.

Jemma was a slender young woman with spiky black hair and looked like she wouldn't weigh more than one-thirty soaking wet. She twisted her wrist and yanked away, putting distance between her and the big man. "Keep your damn hands off me, George!"

She spoke loud and with anger, but Cruz caught the underlying tremor. And why wouldn't she be fearful? The guy was almost three times her size and was surrounded by a bunch of enablers.

"I'm a customer and deserve better treatment," George barked at her, with zero remorse.

She said something indistinguishable to him and then turned on her heel.

George yelled after her. "Go ahead and run to Zeke. He won't do a thing. I spend a lot of money here every week."

The men cackled, and Cruz watched as Jemma rushed toward a back room.

"Some people have no home training. Asshole," Shanice muttered.

Cruz nodded slowly. Most of the occupants in the lounge weren't paying attention, but he was almost crawling out of his skin. There was nothing he hated more than seeing someone being taken advantage of, especially a woman. Hell, that's the reason he'd gotten pulled into Plan B. At the age of eighteen, he landed in jail after beating the crap out of a guy who'd assaulted a woman at a party he'd attended. Working for Plan B had been a more appealing alternative to doing a long stretch behind bars.

A few minutes later, Jemma came back to their table. "Can I get you anything else?" She dodged eye contact.

Shanice leaned forward. "Does that guy come in here a lot and bother you?"

Jemma looked up then. "Yeah, but...I can handle him." Her eyes were red and her voice dull and lifeless. The funny, energetic woman who'd waited on them since they sat down was gone.

"You shouldn't have to," Cruz said.

Jemma swallowed and stared down at the notepad in her hand.

By her demeanor, Cruz had the distinct impression that George had done more than grab her wrist in the bar. Guys like that got off on scaring women. He'd probably waited around for her a time or two after the lounge closed, which meant eventually, he'd move past intimidation and attack her. And since management probably wasn't inclined to help, she was essentially on her own dealing with a three-hundred-pound plus problem.

"Can I get you anything else?" she asked again.

"No, thank you. We had a great time. We'll take the check now," Cruz said.

Jemma removed the printout from her apron pocket and handed it over.

Cruz pulled out his wallet, but his gaze drifted back over to the table of men. He should mind his own business, but he couldn't let them continue harassing her. He just had to figure out how to handle the situation without tearing up the lounge and spoiling Shanice's night out.

The opportunity presented itself when George got to his feet and stretched. He mumbled something to his buddies and then lumbered toward the restroom.

Cruz assessed him as he passed by—noting the faint limp, the baggy jeans, and the way the white shirt stretched across his midsection. He was slow-moving, but taller and wider than Cruz, outweighing him by close to a hundred pounds. But whereas Cruz was all muscle, this guy's body was mostly made up of fat and bad choices.

He and Shanice headed toward the door and nodded

goodbye to Jemma on the way out. In the car, he patted his pockets and groaned. "I left my wallet in there."

Shanice frowned. "Are you sure?"

Cruz was already opening the door. "I'll be right back."

Inside, he went to the table where he and Shanice had been seated. He pulled out the chair and picked up his wallet from where he'd left it so he wouldn't actually have to lie to Shanice. Then he made a beeline for the restroom.

Time to level the playing field.

He pushed open the door. There were only two stalls, and there were two other men in the cramped space with George. One stood next to him at the urinal, and the third man was washing his hands. The one washing his hands looked at Cruz.

"Get out," Cruz said.

The guy knew trouble when he saw it. He immediately turned off the faucet and left.

Cruz pointed at the man beside George. "You, too. Out."

Both he and George looked at him, and the smaller man zipped up his pants and rushed past Cruz through the door. George frowned at him, finished up, and zipped up his jeans.

"I want you to stop bothering Jemma."

The man's eyes swept Cruz from head to toe in a dismissive fashion. "Who the hell are you? Her bodyguard?"

"Yes. She asked you to stop touching her, and you didn't."

George laughed as he let water run over his hands. "I ain't afraid of you."

"You should be."

"Oh yeah?" He smirked and wiped his wet hands on his jeans.

"Yeah."

George approached, hands up in a disarming way. Cruz appeared relaxed but redistributed the weight on his lead foot, ready for the sucker punch he knew was coming.

"Hey man, I don't want no trouble. I hear you. You want Jemma, you can have her..." George swung with his right fist.

Cruz shifted right and blocked the blow with his forearm, following up quick with two savage right hooks to the kidney. A kidney strike was debilitating, and his punches were blisteringly powerful.

George squeaked out a cry and dropped to his knees, face contorting into agony so intense he couldn't release a sound any louder. The bastard would be pissing blood for a while.

Cruz always aimed to end a fight as quickly as possible, so he bashed George's face into the white sink. The big man screamed as the bones in his nose cracked and blood shot from his nostrils. Despite the yell, no one would hear him back here because of the music.

Cruz twisted his arm behind his back and yanked him to his feet by the collar. Time to wrap up this conversation.

"My arm!" George squealed. He sounded like a baby. Not so big and bad now.

Cruz yanked the arm higher at an awkward angle, and George doubled over, pressing his face against the cool sink.

"Shut up or I'll break it." Cruz kept his voice calm, steely.

"What the hell, man." His voice shook with unshed tears.

"Listen carefully—"

The door opened and an older man came in and stopped. He looked at Cruz. He looked at George bent over the sink with a bloody nose. He backed out and let the door close.

Cruz continued. "You're going to keep your hands off Jemma from now on, you got it?"

"Yes," George whimpered.

"I can't hear you." Cruz nudged his arm.

George gasped. "Yes!" he said in a much louder voice. "Please don't break my arm, man. I need it to work."

Cruz didn't give a shit. "You're going to make sure none of your boys harass her, either, *comprendes*?"

"Nobody's gonna lay a hand on her, I promise."

"Don't touch her, and don't verbally harass her, either."

"Not gonna happen on my watch. I promise you that."

Cruz almost busted out laughing but held himself in check, keeping his voice as frigid as an icicle. "One more thing...you and your boys are going to leave her a really nice tip for all the trouble you've caused and all the times you've bothered her while she was trying to do her job. Make sure it's huge, because I'll ask her how much you tipped, and if it's not enough, I'll come get the rest from you."

"Got it, man. Got it."

Cruz let him go and George toppled to the floor on his side and lay there holding his face, immobile and moaning. He'd be in pain for a long time.

Cruz checked his appearance in the mirror. No blood on him anywhere. He straightened his jacket and left the restroom, running into Jemma on the way out.

"Is everything okay?" she asked.

"Yes. I left my wallet, but I have it now." He smiled briefly and patted his pants pocket.

"Awesome. Have a good night."

"You too," Cruz returned, and walked out.

14

Humming to herself, Shanice climbed the stairs and strolled down the hall to the bedroom she and Cruz shared. While he was in the bathroom, she'd gone downstairs for a light snack and carried a handful of caramel popcorn in a plastic bowl. She'd been a snacker before but had the munchies all hours of the night now that she was pregnant.

She entered the dark bedroom and saw Cruz at the window, peering out at the street below. She'd assumed he'd undressed and gotten into bed already but was surprised to see that, like her, he still wore the same clothes from their evening out.

"You make me nervous when you do that. Should I be worried?" she asked.

He turned to face her. "It's a habit I can't shake."

"Not that I mind. I feel very safe with you around, but should I be concerned? Are the neighbors secretly plotting to kill me?" She made light of the topic now, but she'd spent time peering out the windows, too, after believing Nancy Cheng's lie.

"Not that I'm aware of, but I won't let anything happen to you." His deep voice was even lower as he walked slowly toward her.

"I know that."

She could feel herself getting emotional. God, how she loved this man and looked forward to spending many more days and nights with him.

Cruz stopped before her, unsmiling, and took the popcorn from her hands. He placed the bowl on the dresser and then returned to where she was standing. "Do you know how much I love you?" he asked.

"If it's half as much as I love you, it's a lot," she replied, a bit flummoxed by his solemnness.

His left hand came up and cradled the back of her neck. He pressed a gentle kiss to her forehead. "I love you, more than anything or anyone else in this world."

Shanice swallowed, her heart thudding faster at the tone of his voice—the heavy gravity with which he spoke each word.

"You're what I was looking for. What I've needed all along."

"Cruz..."

"Let me say this, because it's not easy for me. I'm usually a man of few words, except when it comes to you, it seems." His sensual lips curved into a smile.

Shanice fell quiet, gazing up into his eyes.

"I wish I could go back in time and find you sooner, so that I could love you longer. But since that's not possible, I plan to make up for wasted time and spend the rest of my days with you, loving you—until death." Cruz lowered to one knee.

Shanice gasped, eyes widening, and slapped her hand against her chest. She hadn't been expecting this. She'd simply thought the romantic evening had inspired his loving words.

He continued to look at her with focused, intense eyes and withdrew his hand from his pocket. Inside his palm was a small black box, which he flipped open, and Shanice gasped again. In the dim light, the emerald-cut diamond solitaire radiated on the platinum band.

"Will you marry me?"

Her eyes filled with tears. Everything she'd dreamed of was happening in quick succession. Cruz was alive, they were starting a family, and now this—*marriage*.

"Yes," she whispered.

He held her trembling hand and placed the ring on her finger. Tears streamed down her cheeks as he stood and cupped her face in his warm palms.

"The day I returned to Islamorada from my mission in Europe, I had this ring with me. I had planned to ask you to marry me, and then the house exploded, and I..." His voice caught, and he swallowed.

"I know. I know." She closed her eyes, commiserating with him on the pain he'd felt—the same pain she'd experienced when she'd seen what she thought was his burned, lifeless body.

"*Te quiero mucho, mi amor*," Cruz said, his voice thick with emotion. "*Quiero pasar el resto de mi vida contigo*." At her questioning glance, he translated, "I want to spend the rest of my life with you."

Shanice flung her arms around his neck. "I want to spend the rest of my life with you, too. I love you so much, baby. I love you so—" The sentence ended prematurely when she pressed her mouth to his. She showered him with kisses—planting them on each corner of his mouth, his chin, his throat. He'd given her what she wanted without asking and made her happier than she ever imagined.

"Oh my goodness, I have to tell my mom!"

Cruz laughed as she rushed over to the nightstand and pulled out her purse. He sat on the bed and she sat on his lap, straddling him as she dialed the number.

"Hello?" Miriam answered groggily. It was after eleven in Arizona, past her mother's bedtime, but she'd fully wake up when she heard the news.

"Mom, guess what? Cruz and I are engaged!"

Her mother screamed, and tears pricked her eyelids as she became overwhelmed with emotion. Cruz brushed away the tears from her lashes with his thumbs.

"That's it. I'll give you the details later. I'm going to hang up now and let you go back to sleep, but I couldn't wait to tell you. I can't wait to see you next month. We have a wedding to plan!"

"Tell Cruz I said welcome to the family!"

"I will."

After they hung up, she repeated the message, and he nodded, staring at her with amusement in his eyes.

"You must think I'm an emotional fool. I feel so silly." Shanice dipped her head and swiped at the last of her tears.

With his hands on her hips, he pulled her closer until her protruding belly pushed against his abs. "Don't. I know exactly how you feel."

"I love you so much."

"I love you, too. More than my own life. I would do anything for you and our baby. Do you understand that?"

Shanice nodded, ducking her head because she was still embarrassed by her overreaction.

"Look at me."

She lifted her gaze.

"*Anything*. You're my life. *Mi vida*." Cruz said. By the fierceness in his eyes, she knew he meant the words.

He kissed her again, his mouth hard against her yielding lips. They rolled onto their sides, and he gently caressed her belly before smoothing his hand up the curve of her back.

They took their time undressing and then made love with gentle, loving caresses. He'd never been this gentle with her. He tenderly kissed her lips, throat, and down the center of her breasts to her bump. He whispered words in Spanish to their unborn child and then continued to travel down her body, pausing to taste the wetness at the apex of her thighs before continuing lower.

His lovemaking was thorough, and she returned the favor, exploring his body as if it was brand new. His beautiful body was like a work of art that had been chiseled with the care of an experienced sculptor.

Cruz settled behind her on his side, and when their bodies joined together, she gasped with pleasure, arching her back into his thrusts. Her soft moans turned into cries of pleasure, and his groans turned into grunts of fiery need. His hand slipped between her legs and massaged her wet clit while his kisses at the back of her neck set her skin aflame.

For the first time ever they climaxed together, bodies trembling as a consuming orgasm swept through their limbs, lifting them high before depositing them on a cloud of sexual fulfillment, exhausted but content.

15

Three and a half years later

"You're going to help me count?" Cruz asked their three-year-old son.

"Yes!" Alexander promised, his voice high with excitement.

Shanice smiled at her little boy, his adoration for his father evident in his dark eyes as he craned his neck to gaze up at him. He had a headful of curly hair that Cruz had wanted to cut six months ago but she'd talked him out of it because she wasn't ready for that stage of his growth yet.

She watched them from the stationary bike, breathing steadily through her mouth as she pumped her legs and sweat cruised down her face. Outside the one-way glass that took up a wall, five men ran practice sprints on the one-mile track.

She'd brought Alex to the Cordoba Agency's gym to spend time with his father while she got in a little exercise. He'd been there so often since he turned one, that all the employees were accustomed to seeing him, and he liked coming to see his "friends," sometimes running around the track with the employees while they practiced and joining in the celebratory high-fives when they did a good job.

Cruz had set up the facility so no one could simply walk in off the street. First, they had to get past the guard stationed at the gate. To enter the main building, each employee had their own security code, and once inside, they remained in a glassed-enclosed foyer until they pressed their hand to the biometric scanner. Inside the state-of-the-art facility were offices, panic rooms, a communications center, and conference rooms. Cruz had also leased a small fleet of late-model SUVs and cars for the company, and he recently signed a contract to add a building with an indoor pool and a hot tub—something he'd put off because he considered it a luxury.

The brightly lit gym contained plenty of equipment to make it easy for the male and female bodyguards to stay in shape. There were stationary bikes, treadmills, cross-trainers, and weights and also a sauna and yoga room.

Business was flourishing, and they were doing much better than Cruz had forecasted, with wealthy clients contracting them for short-term and long-term assignments. With the main campus of the company outside of Atlanta, Cruz set up a public office within the city limits to conduct meetings with potential clients when they didn't visit the client directly. Last month he'd paid off the loan to the billionaire investor, and with all the growth they'd already experienced, he was looking at setting up an office on the west coast to facilitate getting more work from the Hollywood crowd.

Cruz settled their son on his shoulders. "Hang on," he said.

Alex held onto his father's head, and Cruz jumped up to the bar, bent his knees, and crossed his feet at the ankles. Then they started their ritual as he slowly lowered and then pulled himself back up.

"*Uno...dos...*" They counted each time Cruz pulled his chin above the metal bar, Alex very serious and concentrating so he could help his father count.

While lifting weights, Cruz had set aside his charcoal T-shirt and only wore a pair of burgundy basketball shorts. His back and shoulder muscles flexed each time he lifted his fit body higher, a thin sheen of sweat covering his skin from his earlier workout.

After all this time, his strength and agility still amazed her. Her husband was a machine. He didn't go out on many assignments, limiting himself to administrative work or short-term assignments like the local one three days ago, when he and five other bodyguards had been hired to provide additional protection for a visiting diplomat and his family during a twenty-four-hour period. Yet he continued to maintain his body in peak physical condition.

Shanice squirted water into her mouth and started the cooldown phase of her exercise. By the time she was finished, Cruz had completed his reps and Alex was back on the floor.

The toddler raced over. "Mommy, did you see me helping Daddy?"

"I did. You did a great job!"

Proud of himself, Alex did a little happy dance and raced back over to Cruz, who was pulling on his T-shirt.

"You ready to go?" Cruz asked Shanice.

"Yes. Hopefully I can walk." She grimaced and wiped her face with a towel.

"You did good today," Cruz said encouragingly.

"Thanks, baby."

"Daddy, can I be a giant?"

"You want to be a giant? Okay." Cruz lifted Alex back onto his shoulders, but this time instead of sitting down, Alex stood.

This was one of Shanice's least fun ways to see them interact. Cruz was a big man at six-five, which meant Alex had farther to fall than if he were on the average man's shoulders, but she'd grown accustomed to them bonding in ways that made her heart leap into her throat and learned to stay quiet. Her son was fearless, and Cruz wouldn't let any harm come to him.

"Mommy, look at me! Look how big I am. I'm a giant!" With Cruz holding onto his legs, Alex flexed non-existent muscles.

Shanice gave an exaggerated gasp. "Oh my goodness, you *are* a giant."

"Yeah." Alex giggled.

She followed behind them out the door, Cruz having to bend his knees so Alex could clear the doorway. As they walked down the stark white hallway, a male and female bodyguard greeted them with head nods and grinned at Alex, who waved vigorously from his high perch.

They were almost to the door when Alex gasped. "Daddy, I forgot Mr. Cuddles."

Cruz stopped. "Oh no, we can't let you forget Mr. Cuddles."

Mr. Cuddles was the stuffed alligator Miriam had given Alex for his third birthday back in January. He carried it all over the house, and when they went to the store or a restaurant, Mr. Cuddles waited in the car until they returned. He couldn't go anywhere without it.

"I'll get him," Shanice said.

She went back into the gym and saw Mr. Cuddles on the floor near the weights, where Alex had probably abandoned the toy while he "helped" his father.

Shanice picked it up and headed back out to them. The stuffed animal was green with a white belly and stood up on his hind legs. He had a tail that curved around to the front and his teeth were bared in a toothy grin, which looked a little creepy to Shanice because one of his eyes was missing.

Like so many parents, they jumped around in their assessment of what kind of career their son would have later in life. He loved to talk and often added alternate endings to the tales she and Cruz read to him at bedtime. That meant he'd probably be a writer. When he danced around the house, singing at the top of his lungs, or raced around the front yard with Cruz and some of the other kids from the neighborhood, they were convinced he'd become an entertainer or an athlete. His love for that stuffed alligator and desire to touch every single dog he saw meant he was destined to become a veterinarian. The truth was, whatever he decided, they'd be right there, cheering him on.

She met up with Cruz and Alex again. Alex was on the floor while Cruz talked with one of his employees. Alex saw his mother, raced toward her, and grabbed Mr. Cuddles from her hand.

"Thank you, Mommy," he said, hugging the toy.

"You need to take better care of Mr. Cuddles," she scolded him.

"I will. I promise." He hugged the toy tighter.

Cruz ended his conversation and walked the two of them to the car.

As Shanice strapped Alex into the car seat in the back of her gray Honda Accord hybrid, he waved at Cruz. "Bye, Daddy."

"Bye," Cruz said.

Shanice straightened. "Will you be home for dinner?"

"Probably not."

"I'm making meatloaf," she sang. He loved her meatloaf and English roasted potatoes. She usually made two loafs so he could have one for himself.

He groaned and rested his hands on her hips. "I can't. Raheem and I have a video meeting with a potential client in India. If this works out, I'll have to hire some contractors to help us on the project." He sometimes pulled in contractors to help on assignments and had a vetted database of names to pull from.

"Your loss. You can have it for lunch tomorrow." Shanice fisted her hand in his shirt, and he leaned down for her kiss. "If you get in early enough, there's something I want to talk to you about, okay?"

He quirked an eyebrow higher. "This sounds serious."

"It is, but it isn't. It's something we need to discuss. See you later."

She released him and closed the back door.

Cruz smacked her on the bottom, and she spun around, glaring with her eyes but smiling with her lips.

"Cruz!"

He shrugged. "I couldn't help it. You know I can't resist your lovely *culo*." He made a squeezing motion with his hands and Shanice rolled her eyes.

"I'm going to stop coming to see you in the middle of the day because of all the sexual harassment. Go back to work."

He grinned, completely and utterly without remorse, and waved to their son in the back seat, who waved back.

He was still standing outside when she pulled out of the parking lot.

16

S hanice didn't go straight home. She stopped at the library and checked out a book of poetry for herself and several books for Alex. Then they went to the grocery store, where she picked up some additional ingredients for dinner before driving to the new neighborhood where she, Cruz, and Alex resided.

She waved at one of the neighbors—a retired surgeon who was an adjunct professor at Emory University, and then slowed down at the gate in front of their house. She hit the remote on the car's sun visor, and the iron gate slid to the right behind the white brick walls that surrounded the property. Shanice drove into the yard and parked in the driveway instead of the garage.

Few of the houses looked the same around here, and she and Cruz had chosen this one because of its mid-century design—one of only two in the neighborhood, and the only one that had been completely renovated, making it move-in ready. They moved in not long after Alex was born. Cruz wanted a more secure property, and this one included a pool, which he'd wanted so he could continue swimming as exercise.

After they moved out of the house on Rainbow Street, she'd

been a bit down, but she had to admit that she enjoyed their new place more. The mid-century design was like something out of a fifties movie, with high ceilings, an open floorplan, and half the walls covered in windows. There were four bedrooms and three baths, a loft space that overlooked the living room, which they still hadn't figured out what to do with yet, and a pool house with a kitchenette.

Cruz had been so busy working and expanding the Cordoba Agency, she'd had full rein with the interior design. Their house was a stylish mix of contemporary and traditional —creating a visually stunning home.

Shanice entered the kitchen, which was all clean lines with hardwood floors and white cabinets with brass-accented handles. She set the groceries on the tile countertop and quickly prepared a snack of popcorn for Alex while she worked on dinner.

She and Alex went into the living room to eat, where she'd hung a blown-up photo of her and Cruz on their wedding day. The sun was at their backs and Cruz's protective hands on her expanded waistline while he placed a gentle kiss on her exposed shoulder. She'd been surprised and happy the photographer had captured that moment between them. She'd had no idea until the proofs arrived.

The room contained blue and blue-and-white-striped chairs comfortable enough to fall asleep on. She'd been tempted to choose lighter colors, but with a child in the house had gone the more practical route.

She placed their plates and drinks on the coffee table and used the soft area rug as a seat. Alex kneeled on a cushion, and they ate their meal while watching TV. By the time Cruz came home, Alex was already asleep in his Spider-man bed. Shanice was munching on sweet and salty popcorn, her hair in an uptwist, reading the book of poetry she picked up from the library.

When Cruz came into the bedroom, she set aside the book and dusted off her hands. "Hi, babe. How'd your meeting go?"

"Great. Afterward, we emailed the contracts, and I expect we'll have another client before the end of the week." Cruz bent and gave her a quick kiss.

She watched as he went into the walk-in closet and removed his shoes. She needed to broach the topic that had been on her mind for several weeks but wondered if she should wait until tomorrow. The thing was, she didn't want to wait. She had to make a decision soon about the perfect location she'd found for her new idea.

"Before I hit the shower, what was it you wanted to talk to me about?"

"I can wait until you get out of the shower." That gave her more time to work up the nerve to broach the subject.

While Cruz was in the bathroom, she pulled in her legs and wrapped her arms around her knees. She shouldn't be worried. Cruz was reasonable and understanding and open-minded about most things. They'd had very few disagreements over the past few years because he was so laid-back and was satisfied with whatever she wanted, as long as she was happy. But some inner instinct told her he would not be too pleased with the request she'd pose tonight.

Later, when he had exited the bathroom wearing dark pajama pants, he sat down on her side of the bed and said, "Okay, what's going on? I can tell something is bothering you."

He was very perceptive and tuned into her moods.

Shanice slid off the bed and stood before him. "I want you to listen to what I have to say without interrupting, okay?"

He quirked an eyebrow. "Okay."

Shanice took a deep breath. "Things are going great for us. We haven't had to do any work on the house for months, Raheem is on board and your business is doing well, and your hours have leveled off, right?"

Cruz nodded.

"Money-wise, we're in a good place and Alex is thriving and happy. So...I started thinking about what I wanted to do. I know we agreed that I wouldn't work, but I've been thinking a lot lately, and...I'd like to open my own bookstore. I talked to the property manager of the building on Main Street, where the old bookstore used to be, and she said the owner is willing to give me a great deal since he hasn't had anyone leasing there for a while. I won't have much to do, since it was already a bookstore before. I've talked to Beatrice, and she's helped me a lot with the plan and ideas of how to make the business work. I don't want to go out of business like the previous tenant. But I *know* I could make this work. So...what do you think?"

"Where will Alex be when you're at the bookstore?" Cruz's face didn't reveal much.

"He'll be in daycare."

His face immediately darkened. "Shanice..."

"Cruz, this is something for me, okay? I love being a mother, and I love being your wife, but I miss being around books and working with the public. I don't even have to start out full-time. I could start part-time at first and see if business picks up. With the favorable lease terms, I'd have that option. The owner is very flexible. He just wants someone in the building because it's been empty for four years. There are only two other bookstores in Hopevale, and they're both on the other side of town, so there would be very little competition."

"Are you unhappy?"

"No, of course not."

"Then I can't believe we're having this conversation."

Shanice placed her hands on her hips. "What do you mean?"

"Why now? Like you said, everything is going great."

"Why not now? You know I loved working at The Bookish Attic and that books are my passion. Alex is old enough now, he can be in daycare with other kids. He plays with the kids in the neighborhood—"

"While I'm watching. I never let him go off by himself. There are sick people out there who will hurt kids. I'm not taking the chance with my son." Cruz stood and ran his fingers through his hair.

"I know you've seen a lot of bad things in the work you used to do, but you're being unreasonable. You don't have to be so protective of him. He'll be fine. Thousands—millions of kids are in daycare every year."

He shook his head. "Like you said, we had an agreement. I was not put in daycare and my child won't go to daycare. That's final."

"That's *final*? So because you said the conversation is over, the conversation is over?"

"I'm tired. I'm not going to argue with you, Shanice." He walked around to the other side of the bed and pulled down the linens.

"This wasn't supposed to be an argument. I thought we would have a conversation about how I could start a business and we could transition our son into daycare."

"We talked about this before we got married. You were fine being a stay-at-home mother."

"I know that, but I've changed my mind."

"What happens when we have two more kids? Have you changed your mind about that, too?"

"No, I haven't!" she snapped. "But maybe I should, since you seem to think that tying me down so I can't do anything but stay at home is the best way to handle this situation. There's nothing wrong with sending our kids to daycare."

"That won't be happening."

"A nanny then?"

"No."

Shanice slammed her hands on her hips. "Don't do this to me."

He looked at her. "Do what?"

"Give me two- and three-word sentences and expect me to shut up and leave you alone." The times they'd argued, that's how the conversations always ended up. He talked less and she went off on a tangent, as if she were arguing with herself, before his lack of engagement finally took the steam out of her anger.

"You're not changing my mind, so what's the point?"

"You're serious?" She'd expected some resistance, but not this.

"The conversation is over."

They stared at each other across the mattress.

"Well, maybe I'll do it anyway," Shanice finally said.

His jaw muscles tightened. "Don't be ridiculous."

"You mean like you're being ridiculous!" Shanice shouted. She swung on her heel, went into the bathroom, and slammed the door.

"Shanice," Cruz called from the other side. "*Shanice.*" He wiggled the doorknob, but she'd locked it. "Open the door and come to bed."

"You said the conversation is over. Leave me alone." She folded her arms and paced the tiled floor. People changed. Surely he could understand that. Part of being married involved weathering those changes and growing together.

"Come to bed. I'm giving you until the count of three." That sounded ominous.

"Leave me alone! And you better not pick the lock like you did the last time."

Quiet. Then she heard Cruz sigh.

Finally, she didn't hear anything else, and she figured he must have gone to bed. She sat on the edge of the tub with her arms crossed, still fuming. He didn't understand her desire to get back to work. The need was deep inside her, and though she loved having a family, there was a part of her that missed the work she used to do. How could she get him to understand that?

Shanice sat there for a while, ranting to herself. When she finally exited the bathroom, the bedroom was dark, and Cruz was lying on his back. He usually snored, a result of permanent damage to his septum from having his nose broken more than once, so she knew he wasn't sleeping.

He didn't turn or say a word when she climbed into bed and turned on her side away from him. She didn't want to fight with Cruz, but getting back to work was important to her. She didn't know yet how to convince him to change his mind, but she'd think of something.

17

Saturday morning, Cruz woke up with his arm across Shanice's waist. She lay curled on her side in the thin pink sleep shirt she'd worn to bed the night before. He could feel the warmth of her body on his inner arm and against his chest where her back rested against him.

The need to move his hand higher and fondle her breasts was almost unbearable, and he ached to press his hard dick against her plush ass and listen to her contented little moans as he grinded her into arousal. But he knew better. Two nights ago they'd both been angry after their "conversation," and when they woke up the next morning she remained cool toward him. Last night she'd gone to bed before he did and hadn't said goodnight or acknowledged him when he came in after her.

He hated to be *that* guy, the resistant jerk. In most ways, he wasn't and tended to give Shanice anything she wanted. They seldom argued, but when it came to raising his son, he had certain boundaries he wouldn't—couldn't cross, and having someone who wasn't family watching Alex before he reached school age, was one of them. He and Shanice needed to come to an understanding on the topic, particularly since they agreed they wanted to have more children.

His gaze lingered on her exposed arm. The back of her neck tempted him to kiss, and he knew if he pressed his nose he could get a good whiff of her fragrant skin, but he resisted the urge and instead listened to her even breathing in the morning quiet.

Then the door cracked open.

Alex marched over to the bed and tossed up Mr. Cuddles before climbing up after him. With the stuffed animal tucked under his right arm, he crawled over Cruz. Cruz winced as his son's knees dug into his thighs, and he twisted slightly to avoid one of those knees bumping his morning wood. If he hadn't done that, he'd be in a lot of pain right now because his son had no regard for his discomfort and wedged himself between his parents, turning toward his mother. Cruz felt his hard-on die a quick death.

"Well, good morning," he said with some amusement.

"Good morning," Alex mumbled into Mr. Cuddles's face.

Shanice shifted and groaned. "That better not be Alex in the bed this early in the morning."

Her husky morning voice stirred his blood, but his mini-me between them kept any other part of his anatomy from stirring.

The little boy giggled at the mock warning. "Morning, Mommy."

"Good morning, sweet pea." She reached back and patted his leg.

"Mommy, I'm hungry."

"It's too early to be hungry, baby," Shanice mumbled.

"I'm very, very hungry," Alex insisted.

"Mmm, okay. Give me a minute."

"I can fix breakfast," Cruz offered.

"No, I want Mommy to do it." Alex pressed closer to his mother.

"I'll take care of it. I just need to wake up." Shanice yawned.

Seconds later, she rolled out of bed and trudged to the bathroom, and Alex closed his eyes, his arms wound tightly around the stuffed animal.

"Did you have a good night's sleep?" Cruz asked, gently caressing his son's curly hair.

Alex rolled onto his back. "Yes. Me and Mr. Cuddles went on an adventure with Grandma. We went on a long, long drive."

"Where did you go?" Cruz asked, indulgently. Their son had such a vivid imagination. He was convinced he was destined to become a storyteller.

Thinking hard, Alex wrinkled his nose. "To her house?" The answer came out as a question instead of a statement.

"Do you know why you went to Grandma's house?"

He nodded his head. "She was going to give me candy."

"Is that right?" Cruz bit back a laugh. Alex loved candy, but Shanice kept him on a low-sugar diet, which he detested. He whined when he couldn't get any, but she never budged, doling out sweets on very rare occasions.

Alex nodded vigorously. "In the car, she gave me all the candy I wanted. I had red ones, and green ones, and purple ones."

"Wow, that's a lot of candy."

His son's eyes brightened as his face spread into a wide grin. "Grandma always has candy and she always gives me some. I hope she comes to visit soon."

Cruz chuckled. "She'll be back soon, but I'll have to tell her not to give you any more candy."

"No, Daddy, don't tell her that."

"That's exactly what I'm going to do." He tickled Alex, and they ended up in a play fight and getting tangled in the sheets as they wrestled on the bed.

Shanice exited the bathroom wearing her robe, face freshly washed, lips pink and sweet-looking, and her hair brushed, the curls landing in ringlets against her round cheeks and across her forehead. With or without makeup, she was as beautiful as the day he saw her in those photos when Miles came to see him in Islamorada. She stopped at the open bedroom door.

Resting her hands on her hips, she asked, "What do you want for breakfast, Alex?"

"Blueberry pancakes!" he screamed, as if his mother was already in the kitchen instead of standing directly in front of them.

"And what does Daddy want?"

"More time with Mommy," Cruz replied, sending a meaningful gaze in her direction so she understood exactly what he meant.

Her lips flattened. "What do you want for breakfast?" No flirting. She was obviously still upset with him.

"Do we have any more eggs?"

"Yes."

"I'll take eggs and blueberry pancakes."

"Okay. No problem."

"Thank you, *mami*," he said, lowering his voice and shooting her a smile that usually had her returning a smile in his direction.

Nothing. Just a cold stare. He was lucky she was willing to fix him breakfast.

Alex jumped on his chest. "Stop! She's not your mommy, she's my mommy."

"Okay, okay," Cruz said, pretending to be overwhelmed as he blocked the weak blows.

"Breakfast will be ready soon," Shanice announced as she walked away.

Cruz and Alex continued wrestling for a bit longer. Alex jumped on Cruz's back and pounded him with his elbow and Cruz retaliated by tossing him around on the bed and gently beating him with the pillows. The finale came when Cruz got up on his knees and lifted his son in the air, listening to him scream before he body-slammed him on the mattress to the sound of uncontrollable giggles.

"All right, *mijo*, let's get washed up."

He carted the little boy under his arm into the bathroom. They both peed, brushed their teeth, washed their faces, and then went into the kitchen.

As Shanice set the plates and silverware on the table, Cruz poured them each a glass of orange juice, and the three of them sat down at the small table where they often ate their meals. They seldom ate in the dining room, saving that larger space for when they had company.

They held hands and bowed their heads, and Cruz said grace. He and Shanice alternated which one of them said the blessing at each meal. That wasn't something he'd done before they met, but he'd grown accustomed to the practice over the years because of her.

Sunlight poured in through the windows in the kitchen, providing plenty of natural light as they dug into the meal. Alex chattered away as he gobbled the maple syrup-doused pancakes his mother had cut into bite-sized pieces for him, completely comfortable as the center of attention in the midst of their three-person family.

Cruz felt his chest tighten as he watched them. They centered him. Calmed him. Today was normal, regular. Nothing special about it, which was why the day was so perfect.

Even with Shanice being upset with him, he was content and at peace in a way he'd never imagined before.

RANDALL LOGAN SAT on the bed in his small cell at the federal prison in Beaumont, Texas while his cellmate slept on the top bunk. He was staring at the photo of his son taped to the wall, and pain pricked his chest.

Today was the day.

He'd been patient a long time—plotting, bribing. He *couldn't* rest until justice was served.

His son had been loyal and stood by his side when his eldest, Randall, Jr., had abandoned him. He regretted letting Jacob go to DC, believing that his military training and desire to succeed had been enough.

Again, pain lanced through his chest, but it went deeper this time, its bite increased by guilt. He didn't care what he had to do—he would avenge his son's death, no matter the cost.

An inmate pushing the book cart stopped in front of Randall's cell.

"What would you like to read today?" the man asked. He looked much older than his thirty-two years, with sunken eyes and sallow skin.

Using his cane, Randall shuffled over to the bars. "Do you have *War and Peace*? I haven't read the book in ages, and since I have so much time on my hands..." He shrugged nonchalantly.

"Just so happens, I do have a copy." The inmate's voice was even but the direct eye contact he made with Randall was loaded with meaning.

Excellent, the old man thought excitedly.

The inmate handed over the mangled paperback that looked as if it had passed through a thousand hands and been tossed against the wall a thousand times before arriving at his cell.

Randall nodded his appreciation and sent a silent promise with his eyes that he would reward the younger man. He'd been in here since his early twenties, and his girlfriend and son had moved farther away, making trips to the prison few and far between in recent years. He didn't get to see his kid anymore, but Randall had promised to put something on his books and get his girlfriend a car to make the journey easier for her and the boy.

Barely able to contain himself, Randall hobbled over to the small bed and opened the book. Pages had been hollowed out in the center and a folded envelope rested inside. Amazing what could be accomplished in here. He had quickly learned to navigate prison culture, and with the help of a few employees —more loyal to him than his no-good son, Randall, Jr.—had access to money from the business, now being run by his former vice president.

Randall peered over his shoulder to make sure no one was looking. Above him, his bunkmate's low-volume snores indicated he was still asleep. He took out the envelope. Inside were details about a man who'd consumed his thoughts for four years. He hadn't been able to do much during the trial, but he had plenty of time to plot now that he was serving his sentence.

Heart racing, he removed the contents and smiled when he saw the photo and stapled sheets of paper. He flipped through the redacted pages and cursed. There wasn't much information available for him.

He flipped back to the front and read the summary details.

Birthplace: Havana, Cuba
Nationality: U.S. citizen
Languages: English, Spanish
Height: 6 ft. 5 in.
Weight: 260 lbs
Personality: unemotional, lone wolf, natural leader
Skills: Excels at hand-to-hand combat, gun and knife mastery
Notes: Highly intelligent. Prone to violence.

He stared at the name at the top of the first sheet and then lowered his gaze to the passport-sized photo of the man. Dark hair, dark eyes, dark coloring.

Randall decided he didn't need all the other information after all. He was satisfied with what he had. He had a face and a name.

Cruz Cordoba.

The man who murdered his son.

Miriam walked slowly through the building, her eyes sweeping the interior. She was of average height—shorter than her daughter—with bronze-brown skin and a pixie haircut.

Alex walked beside her, also examining the inside of the store.

"Oh, honey, I love it. You have some work to do, though."

A thin film of dust covered the bookshelves and store fixtures, and the industrial carpet was frayed and stained in a few places.

Shanice nodded. "I do, but it's not much, and almost everything I need is already here. After I clean up, I'm going to get a few more shelves and fix up the back office, maybe paint, change the carpet, and that's it. Then I can start ordering books. I'm excited! I'm going to have my own shop!"

"And you've worked in bookstores before, so you know the ins and outs."

"Exactly, and Beatrice has been helpful—giving me tips and lots of advice. She told me to call anytime I have questions."

Miriam clasped her hands together. "All you have to do is get started."

"I know!"

They giggled like school girls and then strolled back to the front with Alex trailing behind them. Outside, Main Street was quiet toward the end of the day, with only a few cars passing by and most of the stores getting ready to close.

Miriam walked behind the front counter and peered into the empty display case while Shanice watched her son spinning in a circle, entertaining himself. "Be careful, sweet pea."

"Okay, Mommy."

Her mother touched her arm and drew her attention. "What's wrong? Something's holding you back, keeping you from completely enjoying this moment."

She'd tried to hide her feelings, but of course her mother saw through the façade. "Seems like my life has been consumed with Alex for so long, and now that I have a different interest, I feel almost...guilty? I don't know." She laughed softly, unsure how to articulate her thoughts.

Her mother's frown lines disappeared and were replaced with a sympathetic expression. "I know exactly how you feel. I was the same way with you."

"How did you handle it? I don't want to abandon him."

"Honey, you're not abandoning him. You have other interests, and that's okay. You're also in a unique position to schedule your life in a way that benefits you and Alex."

"Whoa," Alex said.

He'd stopped spinning and was now giggling and dizzily spreading out his hands to keep his balance. Shanice rushed over and held him so he wouldn't fall. "That's enough, mister."

When he'd calmed down, he pointed to a stack of empty cardboard boxes. "Can I play over there?"

"Yes, but be careful." Alex started stacking the boxes on top of each other, the way he did his toy blocks. Shanice returned her attention to her mother. "You were saying?"

"I was saying you're in a unique position right now because you're going to start a business, which means you can do what a lot of parents can't. You can send Alex to daycare, but set your shop hours so that you can still spend part of the day with him."

Shanice shook her head. "Daycare is out. Cruz is completely opposed to the idea and untrusting of daycare workers. We had a fight a couple of weeks ago about the whole thing, and he says he wasn't put in daycare and doesn't want his son going. We talked about it again, and my only option is to bring him to work with me. That's what we decided because my hard-headed husband won't budge."

Miriam folded her arms cross her chest. "That could work, I guess, but some days you're going to need a break. How are you going to manage the store and wrangle a three-year old every day?"

"I could hire help, I guess."

"He'll still be underfoot."

Shanice sighed. "I don't know what to do, and we want to have more kids."

"Cruz won't even consider letting someone watch Alex? What about a part-time sitter?"

"No. He's not budging on this topic, and in his defense we had agreed that I would be a stay-at-home mom. He didn't have any problem reminding me of that, and he actually said, 'that's final' to me." Shanice rolled her eyes.

They stood in silence for a bit, both of them watching Alex as he played. Once he'd stacked the boxes, he knocked them down and squealed and clapped before he started piling them on top of each other again.

"Maybe Cruz is right, that I should wait. We can have two more kids, like we discussed, and once they're all school age, I can open the store." She glanced at her mother to gauge her reaction.

Miriam pursed her lips. "That means your dream of owning your own bookstore is years away, and someone else might come along and take this spot."

Shanice shrugged. "It's not the end of the world. Marriage is about compromise, right? Cruz gave up the work he loves to settle down with me, so I can give up something, too, to make our marriage work. He doesn't ask for much and gives me whatever I want. I really can't complain. This is one thing."

"Sounds like you're trying to convince yourself," her mother said dryly.

"I want you to agree with me and tell me I'm making the right decision, instead of doing what I want to, which is throttle my husband while he sleeps."

Her mother laughed. "It's not a *wrong* decision. Lots of women make the choice you have, but are they happy?"

"Lots of women choose to have a career and a family, and they're not happy, either."

"There has to be balance in everything you do. For you, that balance comes from being around books. You've always been that way, ever since you were a kid. You spent so much time at the library, I used to worry until your father pointed out that it was a good thing. Better than you getting into trouble." She laughed, her eyes clouding over. "Gosh, I miss that silly man."

Shanice squeezed her mother's arm. She sometimes had moments like that, too, when she thought about something her father did or said and then the sadness washed over her at the memories.

"Anyway, my point is, you're a book lover. It's in your blood. Didn't come from me, because you're the one who influenced me to start my book club."

"You mean your party club."

"We do have a good time." Miriam laughed. "Here's a

thought, and tell me what you think about this. If I lived nearby, I could help you watch Alex until he starts school. What do you think?"

"Mom, I love the idea, but...are you sure? You're going to leave all your friends in Arizona?"

"I can make more friends and start another party book club. You're my family, and to be honest, I miss you and Alex and Cruz when I'm gone. And when you have more kids, you'll need more help and I could be here."

Shanice loved the idea and knew Cruz wouldn't mind. He spoke fondly of his grandmother and her influence on him, and he adored her in the same way Alex adored Miriam.

"By the time we have another baby, I might be in a position to at least have some help at the store so I could take a break and cut my hours with the new baby."

"True. I didn't work until you were two, and then I started part-time, and eventually went-full time when you started pre-school."

"Mom, I think this could work."

"I know it can," Miriam said smugly.

"Thank you!" She gave her mother a quick hug. "You solved the problem just like that." She snapped her fingers.

"I know, honey. That's what mothers do."

"Oh boy. I've created a monster."

They both laughed.

"I'll run the idea by Cruz tonight. Ready to get some dinner?"

"I sure am. I liked those big salads we got at the diner the other day."

"Ooh, those were so good. Want to go back there?"

"Definitely."

"Okay. I think I'll get the steak and blue cheese salad this time, though. Would you get Alex and put him in the car while I lock up?"

"No problem. Come on, Alex." Miriam extended her hand and he rushed over but looked back at Shanice questioningly.

"I'll be right there. I have to turn out the lights and lock up."

"Okay, Mommy."

As they exited, Shanice went to the back and turned out the lights. Her mother's idea was a great one, and it would be nice to have her nearby. She'd discuss the idea with Cruz first, though she didn't doubt he'd be okay with it. She couldn't think of any legitimate objection. He'd certainly like the idea better than sending Alex to daycare. Yes, her mother's idea was a viable alternative.

Shanice was walking slowly toward the front when she heard a panicked scream of "No! Stop!"

That was her mother's voice.

"*Stop! Help!*" Her mother's voice again, louder this time and more frantic.

Shanice raced toward the front of the store and burst out the door. Miriam scrambled to her feet and ran in the direction of a dark brown SUV that was tearing down the street.

"Alex!" she screamed, coming to an abrupt stop as the vehicle narrowly missed a man and his dog, who had to race to the opposite side of the road to avoid getting hit.

"Mom, what—" Shanice stared at the open car door and the empty car seat. No Alex. No Mr. Cuddles.

The heat of the dying sun suddenly seemed extra hot and its glow overly bright. Her stomach tightened as terror seeped into her brain. She couldn't move. She stood there, frozen, unwilling to believe her own eyes.

Miriam swung in her direction, her eyes wide and face filled with horror. Then she brought her hands to her mouth, as if covering a silent scream.

Shanice rushed over and gripped her mother's arms. "What happened?"

"They t-took him."

"Who? Who took Alex?"

"Two men. I was strapping him in when they pulled up. Before I knew what was happening, one of them jumped out of the SUV, shoved me down, and took him right out of the seat." Her voice cracked and she started shaking uncontrollably. "Oh my god. Oh my god, Shanice. They took our little Alex!"

19

C ruz reclined in his leather chair, arms on the rests as he chatted with Raheem, seated across from him.

He'd gone the traditional route when he decorated his office. While Raheem's had a more modern décor filled with glass and monitors, he had chosen overstuffed guest chairs, a brown leather sofa that faced a table and a mostly empty bookcase built into the wall, and a sturdy, heavy oak desk that his crossed ankles rested on.

During the days Water of Life Ministries was operational, this used to be the pastor's office, so it was quite spacious, and if he looked out the window behind him, he saw the front gate, the road leading to it, and much of the parking lot.

The position of the office had been perfect, but Cruz had made a few changes to its interior. He decreased the square footage by building a small room behind a false wall. It could be accessed using a secret lever behind one of the books on the shelf. The bookcase would then spring forward enough for him to pull it open to reveal the door. The small room could be used as a hiding place, but its main purpose was as hidden storage for his weapons of choice—several handguns and ammunition, an AR-15 and its ammunition, and a number of KA-BAR knives. He hoped he'd never have to use them here, but he liked to be prepared.

Cruz threw his head back and laughed at Raheem's story about how he'd pretended not to speak English to avoid getting pummeled when the husband of a woman he'd been seeing came home early from a work trip.

"Come on. You expect me to believe that he bought that?" Cruz said.

"Man, I'm telling you the truth," Raheem said. He put a hand over his heart and held up his left hand. "He bought her story that I was there to fix the computer. Thank goodness I'd brought in my tools as a cover so the servants wouldn't question why I was there."

"He didn't question the fact that your shirt was unbuttoned and you were barefoot?"

"He didn't say another word to me because he thought I couldn't speak English. Maybe he said something to her after I got the hell outta there. After that, I told myself I'm never messing with another married woman again."

As the laughter died down, Cruz thought once again about how much he appreciated Raheem joining him in this endeavor. Three years in, and the business was flourishing, and much of that was because of his friend's technological acumen. Times like this, when they were shooting the breeze at the end of the day before going their separate ways, made him appreciate this period in his life. Though at times he missed the excitement of carrying out an operation, he liked the stability of having a family now and a friendship and partnership he could count on.

"Glad you learned your lesson," he said.

"Hey, if there's one thing I can tell you, I do learn my lesson." Raheem sat forward. "So, have you and Shanice figured out what you're going to do about Alex once she opens her store?"

Cruz bristled but replied, "We talked about it again the other day, and I told her how I feel."

"Come on, Cruz. That's old-fashioned, and you know it."

"I don't care if it's old-fashioned. I don't want my son being raised by strangers."

"It'll be good for him to get acclimated to other kids."

"He can do that with the kids in the neighborhood. A couple across the street has four children. We've gotten to know the family and they love Alex."

"What are you going to do when Alex starts school?"

"That's different."

"Shanice still hasn't changed her mind, either?"

"We've reached an understanding. She's going to open the store, but Alex will be with her during the day."

"Goddamn, Cruz." Raheem picked up a square-shaped paperweight made of blue glass. The company name and logo were engraved on one side. "You know, I just had a thought," he said, bouncing the paperweight from one hand to the next.

"I'm not changing my mind, Raheem," Cruz said.

"Hear me out. What if when Shanice opens the store, you guys take turns with him during the day. He could spend some of his days with us."

Cruz frowned, tapping the right armrest with his thumb. "I don't know..."

"He likes being here, right? When Shanice needs a break, he could hang out with you or with me in the comm room. You know I don't mind having my godson around. He could eat lunch with us and the rest of the guys, and he loves to work out —at least he thinks he's working out when he goes to the gym." Raheem laughed. "And if you're worried about his safety, there's no safer place than right here, behind the locked doors of the

Cordoba Agency." Raheem lifted his eyebrows, daring Cruz to contradict his point.

"You know...you might be right. It wouldn't be a hassle for him to spend the day with me sometimes. I'll have to run it by Shanice, but I think she'd like the idea." Cruz's cell phone rang, and he glanced at the screen. "This is her now." He answered the phone. "Hello, my love."

Raheem stuck a finger in his mouth and pretended to gag. Cruz shot him the finger.

"Cruz! Ohmigod, baby. They took him. They took him!"

Her panicked words raised the hairs on the back of Cruz's neck. He dropped his feet to the floor and straightened in the chair. "Shanice, slow down. Who took who?"

Sobbing, she answered, "Someone kidnapped Alex from right in front of the store and drove away."

"What!" Surely he'd misunderstood what she said.

Frowning, Raheem leaned forward. "What's wrong?"

Cruz hopped to his feet as tension tightened in his body. "Tell me everything. What did you see? What did the vehicle look like?"

"I-I didn't see much. I was inside the store, but Mom was outside with Alex. I heard her scream, and when I came out, I saw a brown SUV driving away. She said they took Alex. They were gone so fast and far away, I didn't get to see the license plate number. I would have remembered it if I'd seen the license plate!"

"I know, I know. Calm down, *mami*. What else can you tell me?" His gaze connected with Raheem's. His friend was frowning up at him.

"I don't know anything else. I—" She broke off when her mother said something in the background.

"Let me talk to your mother," Cruz said in a crisp voice.

Miriam came on the line. "I'm so sorry, Cruz." Her voice shook and tears thickened her words.

"Listen to me, don't blame yourself. Just tell me what you saw. I'm going to place you on speaker so that Raheem can hear you, too."

He hit the Speaker icon, and they both listened as she explained what happened outside the store. Cruz felt his stomach tighten as she mentioned how they'd shoved her down and grabbed his son from the seat. How he'd screamed for her, clutching his stuffed animal, as the man dived into the open back door and they sped away.

"I can still hear his cries," Miriam sobbed, her words almost unintelligible as she wept.

"Put Shanice back on the phone," Cruz said. He didn't have time to comfort her at the moment. That could come later. Right now, they had to act fast.

"Hello?" Shanice sniffled.

"Did you call the police?"

"Not yet. I called you first."

"As soon as we hang up, call the police. I'm on my way."

"Hurry, baby. I need you."

"I'll be there soon." Cruz hung up.

"Holy shit. Are they trafficking kids from Hopevale, Georgia?" Raheem asked.

Cruz swallowed the bile that bubbled in his throat. He didn't want to think about that type of scenario. Human trafficking rivaled the drug and gun trade in revenue, and while the children forced into sexual slavery and domestic servitude were often older, it was not unheard of for traffickers to sell children as young as Alex.

"It's not that farfetched. We're very close to Atlanta, and it's been a hub for human traffickers for years because of the busy airport and the four major interstates that run through the city."

"Yeah, you're right." Raheem ran a hand over the back of his head.

Cruz grabbed his keys from atop the desk. He had to get out of there, and he had to keep his mind from going in the direction it had started in. He didn't want to think about the sickos looking for young kids to exploit. "I need to get to the scene, see if there are any clues left behind, and find out what any witnesses might have seen while the details are fresh in their minds."

A fierce light came into Raheem's eyes. "I'm coming with you. That's my godson out there."

Cruz nodded his acceptance and appreciated the additional eyes and ears he'd have with Raheem there.

His phone rang again, and he glanced down at the device in his hand. *Private* flashed on the screen. A knot of unease formed in Cruz's stomach, but he lifted the phone to his ear.

"Hello?"

"Hello, Cruz. How are you today?" The man's voice was vaguely familiar.

"Who is this?" he asked sharply, searching the far recesses of his mind to recall who it belonged to.

"You don't remember me? Am I really so forgettable?"

"*Who is this?*" Cruz repeated.

The man laughed. "I'll give you a hint. Four years ago, you killed my son. Now I'm going to kill yours."

The air was sucked out of the room, and Cruz's grip on the phone slackened to the point that he almost dropped it. His gaze met Raheem's curious frown a few feet away.

Cruz gulped down the fear that tightened his throat and threatened to choke him. There was only one answer to that riddle. Only one person from his past fit within the confines of the given clues.

Randall Logan.

20

"Are you still there, Mr. Cordoba?"

Logan knew his first and last name and had his phone number. How was that possible?

He hit the Speaker icon so Raheem could listen in again. "If you hurt a single hair on my son's head, I will—"

"You will what?" The question dripped with disgust. "You can't touch me in prison, and you don't know who has your son. Those men are long gone now."

"I've tracked down men with less information."

"I'm sure you have, but that's of little interest to me."

"Did you call to gloat?"

"Yes. Yes, I did. And—"

"I'm going to fucking kill you and everyone involved in kidnapping my child—"

The line went dead.

Cruz stared at the phone and then let out a roar of fury. He tossed the phone to the carpet and slammed the side of his fist on the desk. Then he kicked the base of it so hard that pain zigzagged up his leg and a segment of wood broke off and fell onto the carpet.

"Fuck." He tunneled the shaky fingers of both hands through his hair. "I'm going to kill that motherfucker." He cursed Logan and his whole family in a stream of profanity-laced Spanish.

Raheem picked up the phone. "When we figure out who has Alex, I'll help you put a bullet in every one of those bastards myself, but right now we have to get to Shanice and Miriam, okay? Let's do that. I'll drive."

Numbly, Cruz nodded. His friend was right. He needed to keep his wits about him and not let emotion override his instinct to act with the logic and intelligence that had been honed from years of experience. But every time he thought of his son—his laughing, sweet-faced boy—an ache filled his chest. If they hurt him. *Jesus.*

The phone rang again, and they both froze. Cruz stared at the cracked screen in Raheem's hand. Once again, the number was not visible. *Private.*

With stomach muscles rigid from anxiety, he took the device from his friend and answered by turning on the speaker phone again. "Hello."

"Are you calm now?"

Cruz gritted his teeth. Nothing would give him more plea-sure than to tear that old bastard into pieces with his bare hands.

He took two calming breaths. "Yes."

"Good. Because I'm the one in control here, not you." Logan paused, as if making sure those words landed and were digested. "Now that we've established who's in charge, I know you're worried about your son, your flesh and blood. Like I was worried about my son."

"Your son wasn't a three-year-old innocent little child."

"He was still my son!" Randall snarled. "And you took him from me. I should do to yours, what you did to mine. Kill him. Put a bullet in his right eye and leave his body in the street. I saw the pictures, Mr. Cordoba. Would you like to see the pictures of your dead son?"

Raheem shook his head, sending Cruz a silent message to stay calm.

Unable to remain standing, Cruz collapsed on one of the two chairs, and Raheem stood beside him. He rested a hand on Cruz's shoulder and squeezed.

"What do you want? You want something," Cruz said.

"You're right, Mr. Cordoba. I do want something. I want you. I will spare your son's life if you turn yourself in to me. Do we have a deal?"

"Yes," Cruz answered without hesitation.

Cool, arrogant laughter came through the line. "I thought you would agree. I know I don't have to tell you this, but don't do anything stupid like involve law enforcement to help you. If I get even a whiff of the police or the FBI getting involved, I'll have your boy killed and buried where you'll never find him, and that's a promise. Within twenty-four hours, one of my men will be in touch with the details of where, when, and how we will make the trade—your life for your son's. I assure you, Mr. Cordoba, these men are dangerous and kill without remorse. If I were you, I'd follow their instructions to the letter if you want to see little Alexander alive again. And then I will have the pleasure of watching them kill you. It won't bring back my son, but your death will go a long way toward balancing the scales of justice."

Logan hung up, and several seconds passed before Cruz could move. Tears pushed to the back of his eyes. He'd faced down armed men with the odds stacked against him, yet he had never felt so helpless and scared in his life. Alex wasn't dead, and he had to keep that in mind. But if anything happened to him... Nausea roiled his stomach and he quickly abandoned the direction of his thoughts.

"You can't go along with what he said. You can't let them swap you for Alex," Raheem said.

Cruz lifted his gaze. "I don't have a choice, Raheem."

"You know you can't trust this guy. What if he kills you *and* Alex?"

Cruz shook his head. "He wants me. The man who killed his son. He wants the satisfaction of watching me die."

Raheem muttered a mild curse and ran a hand down his face. "What are you going to do?"

"Do we have anyone at that prison? If I remember correctly, Logan's at Beaumont in Texas."

"I don't think so."

"Find out. Get on the phone with Miles. I'm sure he knows someone. Find out everything you can about Logan's situation in prison. What privileges does he have? What kind of protection does he have set up? He's a cop-killer, so he must have protection, at least from the guards. Who supplied him with the phone to make the call? Anything at all that you can learn, I want to know it."

"Done."

With renewed strength, Cruz stood. He couldn't save his son by being weak. He had to think. He only had twenty-four hours or less to devise a plan before the call came through.

"I need to put a team together. I want the best of the best."

"Some of our old Plan B crew?"

Mind racing, Cruz nodded. "We need a sniper. Do you know where Mouse is?"

"I can find out."

"Call Sanchez and find Hunter. Last I heard he was living a life of leisure on the French Riviera. I want Alissa, too. She's the best driver I know. Tell them I'll double whatever their fees are. Then I'll need a few other guys—mercenary types. No more than four." He was planning blind but through past experience knew that wherever the meeting point would be, they were better off with a small, lethal force to decrease the chance of detection. "None of our guys from the Cordoba Agency. I want to keep this separate from the business. Tell them I'll pay their fees up front if they can be here in twelve hours. We should have a few empty beds in the dorm, and I'll find somewhere to put any extras."

He swallowed. He felt better now that a plan was formulating.

"While you work on that here, I'll go meet Shanice and her mother to collect whatever information I can at the scene."

Raheem clapped him on the shoulder. "Don't worry, I'll take care of everything on this end."

"Only the best, Raheem."

"You got it."

They paused, looking at each other, both probably thinking the same thing. They were dispassionate about killing. That's why they were good at their jobs. They successfully executed their plans with ease because there was no emotion involved.

This would be much more difficult. Without another word, Cruz left, with the knowledge that this would be his most difficult mission to date.

21

The police were already at the bookstore when Cruz arrived. Two patrol cars were parked in front, and people hovered nearby and more across the street, whispering and talking amongst themselves, faces filled with a combination of concern and curiosity.

He parked parallel to the sidewalk in front of a flower shop and then walked toward the gathered group. His gaze swept the area as he approached, noting which stores were open and which ones weren't, watching each person standing around—checking for any suspicious behavior beyond normal curiosity.

Shanice and Miriam were in conversation with a male officer. Two other officers, one female, one male, kept the onlookers at bay.

Shanice saw him first. "Cruz!"

He didn't hear his name, but her lips moved, whispering the words as relief flooded her red-rimmed eyes. She pushed past two onlookers and rushed to him.

He immediately folded her in his arms, absorbing as much of her tension and fear as he could.

"I'm so glad you're here," she whispered into his shoulder.

Cruz rubbed her back and neck, holding her in a tight, comforting embrace.

Finally, she took his hand and led him to where her mother and the officer stood. Miriam's eyes were also red-rimmed, her mouth downturned, and her arms wrapped around her body, like someone underdressed in thirty-degree weather.

"This is my husband, Cruz Cordoba," Shanice said, introducing him to the officer.

"Hello, Mr. Cordoba. I'm Officer Tuffin," the man said, in a deep voice. He was of average height, thick-bodied, with a bushy, untrimmed black moustache that completely covered the space between his nose and upper lip.

"You can call me Cruz."

They shook hands, and then Cruz rested a hand on Miriam's shoulder.

She looked up at him with a forlorn expression in her eyes. "I should have moved faster. I should have done something different. I wish..." Her lower lip trembled.

Cruz gave her shoulder a reassuring squeeze. "You can't blame yourself. These people came out of nowhere and pushed you down and snatched Alex. They were professionals. You couldn't have stopped them."

"I should have done something else. I could have fought more." Miriam chewed on her upper lip.

"Mom, stop it." Shanice released Cruz's hand and stepped over to her mother. She wrapped her arms around her. "We'll find him, and he'll be fine." Her gaze met Cruz's, seeking confirmation.

"We'll get him back." He turned to the officer. "What information have you gathered so far?"

Men tended to like talking to other men—mechanics, plumbers, businessmen, police officers. Whenever another man entered the scene, their attitudes changed and they shared more information. Cruz took advantage of this knowledge by going to stand beside Officer Tuffin instead of facing him directly. In such a way, he gave the illusion of intimacy while allowing the officer to feel non-threatened and thus more likely to divulge information.

Officer Tuffin straightened his shoulders and his voice deepened. "So far, we don't have much, other than what your wife and mother-in-law told us. The men moved quickly, and the only other witness was a man walking his dog, who almost got run over. Thanks to him, we have a partial plate along with the description of the vehicle. We also have this..." He walked into the cordoned off street and pointed to skid marks on the road.

Cruz took several photos with his phone and entered the license plate numbers into the memo app.

"That's all we have for now," Officer Tuffin said. "We put in a call to the Atlanta police to get their forensics team out here. We're a small police force, without the technology and access they have, but they should be here shortly to help."

"Any cameras in the area?" Cruz scanned the street.

"There's one at the bank." Officer Tuffin nodded in that direction.

Cruz made a note of the bank branch. He'd have Raheem look into it.

"Thank you, officer. Anything else you can think of?"

Officer Tuffin shook his head regretfully. "There's not that much evidence here. Classic snatch and grab, and like you said, they were pros."

From his own cursory observation, Cruz agreed there wasn't much evidence available. He already knew who the culprit was, but he'd hoped that he'd be able to gather information that would lead them to the kidnappers *before* the call came in. He'd wanted a head start, but he wouldn't get it here, that was clear.

"Thank you. Do you have a card?"

The officer handed him one.

"I'm going to take my wife and mother-in-law home now, if you're done questioning them...?"

"Yes, we're all done. I have your wife's number if I think of anything else."

"Good. Please give us a call if there are any developments. In fact, you can call me directly." He gave his number, and the officer wrote it down. "I'll take them home now."

"I think that's a good idea."

Cruz went back over to where both women were standing and told them they'd be leaving.

"What about the car?" Miriam asked.

"We'll need to leave it. Forensics is coming from Atlanta and they'll want to examine it," Cruz answered.

"I don't think we should leave," Shanice said.

"You can't do anything here, and I need to talk to you both about a development." He shepherded them toward his SUV, and they all climbed in—Shanice beside him and her mother strapped into the back.

They rode in silence for a few minutes before he told them about the phone call with Randall Logan, leaving out the part where Logan threatened to kill Alex. When he was finished, Shanice stared at him in stunned silence, and Miriam sat back and groaned, covering her face with one hand.

Cruz maneuvered down the street toward their house.

"All this time he's been plotting revenge?" Shanice asked in disbelief.

"Apparently."

"But he's a criminal! He murdered Dennis to hide his scheme to take over those apartment complexes. He had police officers killed. Not to mention the only reason his son is dead is because you had to kill him because he had a gun to my head and threatened to kill *me!*"

"He doesn't see what happened the same way we do. I killed his son, and that's all he cares about. Now he wants me in exchange." Cruz waited as the metal gate to their house opened.

"What are you going to do?" Shanice asked in a small voice.

"I'm going to meet them as soon as the call comes in."

"Should we call the police? The FBI?" she asked hesitantly.

"No. I'm not taking the chance that Logan will find out, or even worse, that they'll screw up the rescue. I can handle this. I'm going to get our son back."

THE CALL CAME IN LATE, at almost two in the morning. Raheem had decided not to drive back to his place in Atlanta and was asleep in one of the dorm beds. Miriam was at the house. She'd wanted to come to the facility, but Cruz and Shanice had insisted she remain at home. As a precaution, Cruz stationed two bodyguards there with her. Last they'd checked, she'd finally fallen asleep.

Neither Cruz nor Shanice could sleep, though. They were both in Cruz's office on the leather sofa. Cruz was wired and used a notepad to scribble ideas and sketch out his plans. Shanice sat shoulder to shoulder beside him, unable to add anything to the process but simply needing to be close and stay involved.

When the phone rang and Cruz saw the private number, his gut tightened.

"This is them," he said.

Shanice sat up straight and gripped his right biceps in both hands, and he answered the phone on speaker so she could hear the conversation.

"Mr. Cordoba?" a voice said. It wasn't Logan this time. This man sounded younger.

"Yes."

"No weapons, no law enforcement. You're allowed to bring

one person to collect your son, that's it. You'll need to be at the following location at five p.m."

Instead of an address, he gave GPS coordinates, and Cruz wrote them on the notepad.

"Can I speak to my son? I need to know that he's all right."

"No." The line went dead.

"Son of a...!" Cruz's grip on the phone tightened and a stream of curses flew from his mouth.

Shanice's two-handed grip tightened. "Do you think he's still alive?"

"Yes," he answered. He needed to believe that.

Shanice nodded, but the fear in her eyes twisted his gut.

"I'm going to call Raheem. We don't have much time, and I don't know where this is. We only have..." Cruz glanced at his watch. "Fifteen hours to get ready and get there."

"It's not enough time," Shanice whispered.

"It's enough time." Cruz brought his face level with hers. "Have you already forgotten who I am?"

"I know who you are, and I know I shouldn't worry, but it's been more than three years since you've had to complete a dangerous mission, Cruz, and this one is involving our baby. I'm so...nervous. Scared. I trust you, but I can't help it."

"I'll get him back."

"And what about you?" Shanice flung her arms around him. "Please be careful. Please."

"I will," he promised.

22

Cruz stood with Raheem at the front of the communications room. The recessed lights were low and the main wall had turned into a big screen that displayed a satellite image of the property matching the GPS coordinates, a newly-erected two-story building in a clearing in the Smoky Mountains of Tennessee.

From the intel they'd already gathered, it was the location for a small but aggressive PMC named The Custer Brigade that was building a reputation for themselves. Most recently, they'd been contracted by a mining company to rescue executives who'd been held for ransom in South America, but their ultimate goal was to get a lucrative U.S. government contract.

Heat sensors on the drone Raheem had sent over the property showed seventeen persons on site, but that number would likely increase at the time of the exchange. There was only one road into the property, which meant they'd have to approach on foot to avoid being seen. There were no cameras detected in the woods, and with no fence surrounding the property, it was clear they'd chosen that spot for its seclusion.

Cruz and Raheem took their time explaining the plan to

their small audience. There were three rows of tables, each with computers spread out across its surface and chairs in front of them. Shanice didn't sit at any of the tables. She sat in the very back on a chair Cruz had brought in for her.

They hadn't had a lot of time to pull together a plan, but he believed in the current strategy. He had shared the team's files with Shanice to put her mind at ease, and she'd been impressed with their abilities. From the quick overview she'd done and the information he had given her, she now had a general understanding of why he had assembled these specific people.

Everyone had arrived in record time. Some sat in the chairs in front of the computers, others stood, but they all wore determination on their faces. Raheem had recruited four mercenaries—two former Navy SEALs and two former Rangers for the mission. But as far as Cruz was concerned, they were backup. The main team was made up of five people, including Raheem, all former Plan B compatriots.

"Mouse, you're going to set up here." Cruz placed the laser pointer on a spot that had heavy foliage that could provide the cover needed.

Kinsey was the youngest and the smallest—hence the name "Mouse." A fair-skinned Black woman with the same complexion as Shanice, she was a sniper and parkour expert, though her shooting ability was what he would make use of today. She sat at the front, her hair cut short and lying brushed flat on her head.

"Got it," she said, nodding, face set in hard lines as she paid attention to Cruz's instructions that followed.

"What vehicle do you have for me?" Alissa asked.

She was the only other woman—with dark brown skin, an oval face, and high cheekbones. She grew up on the island of St. Thomas in the U.S. Virgin Islands, spoke with accented English, and wore her black, natural hair in a bun on top of her head. If you were in a tight spot in the air, on land, or in the sea and needed a clean getaway, you called Alissa. She could maneuver a helicopter or boat under extreme circumstances, but her true gift was driving a getaway car. They used to joke that she learned that skill growing up on a tiny island where the roads were narrow and treacherous. He wouldn't trust anyone else to get his son safely out of the compound.

"Four-wheel drive is all I need. You get me a sturdy Jeep and no one can stop me."

"Done. Any other questions?"

"Are you trying to take down the whole building?" a Spanish-accented voice asked.

That was Alejandro Sanchez—or as everyone called him, Sanchez—an explosives expert. The Mexican stood in the middle of one of the rows, arms crossed over his chest. Needing a shave, he looked ungroomed and there were circles under his eyes, but Cruz was appreciative that he had arrived. Now that he knew what they were dealing with, Sanchez had become an integral part of the plan.

"Once we grab their drives and any other intel, I want nothing left but embers," Cruz replied.

A smile of pleasure expanded on the Mexican's lips. "*Sin problemas, amigo,*" he said.

"Any other questions?" Cruz asked, his gaze traveling over the group.

They all shook their heads, including Hunter, who sat with his feet propped on a table in the front row. Surprisingly, he was the first to arrive. He wasn't in the south of France as originally thought. He was actually in Pennsylvania, having recently wrapped up a job. What Cruz needed from him was his sharpshooting ability.

"Where will I be?" Shanice asked from the back. Silence filled the room, and a couple of heads turned to look at her.

"You'll be in a different location. You won't be on site," Cruz answered. "All right, if there are no more questions, I want all of you to get some rest because—"

"What do you mean I won't be on site?" Shanice was standing now, staring at him in disbelief.

He looked steadily at her. "We'll discuss this after the meeting."

This time the quiet in the room was awkward, and the team members averted their eyes. No one said a word in the weighted silence.

She sat down and crossed her arms over her chest, a mutinous set to her mouth.

Cruz finished the closing remarks and then dismissed the group. When they were all gone, including Raheem, he walked to the back and stood over Shanice.

"You're not coming to the site, Shanice."

"Do you really think you can keep me from seeing my son safely returned?"

"I'll have Alissa or one of the men bring him to you. I don't want you there. It's not safe."

She jumped to her feet. "Then tie me to a chair! Because short of that, I'm coming!" Shanice screamed back at him, shaking.

"Dammit, Shanice." He let the finality in his voice convey that he was seriously considering tying her to a chair, like she suggested.

Her brown eyes widened in panic and she clutched the front of his shirt. "Please, Cruz, you have to let me come. That's my baby. I have to see him, I have to know that he's okay. And he might be scared and need me. *Please.*"

Cruz huffed out a breath and ran a hand down his face in frustration. "I don't like this."

"I won't be any trouble. Give me a gun, if you want. I know how to use one. You know I've been practicing."

Cruz didn't like the idea of her being onsite *at all*. There were too many variables to consider, and if anything went wrong, she'd be in danger. But he didn't want her worrying about Alex unnecessarily, and her pleading eyes were his undoing.

"All right," he said with deep reluctance.

Shanice let out a relieved breath and flung her arms around his torso. Resting her cheek against on his chest, she whispered, "Thank you."

"On one condition," he added.

He could feel her holding her breath. She lifted her gaze to his.

"You stay back where it's safe, where you can see the exchange. One of the men will take you to meet Alissa and Alex once he's safely in the Jeep, is that understood?"

She nodded vehemently in agreement. "Are you going to give me a gun?"

"No."

He'd given her lessons at the firing range at the Cordoba compound. She didn't practice regularly like he and his staff did, but she'd improved a lot. Still, she was uncomfortable with the weapon, stating on more than one occasion that she hoped she'd never have to use one. He'd told her numerous times she might be surprised what she was capable of if she was in a dangerous situation, but her insistence that she wasn't sure she could pull the trigger made him decide he would not give her a weapon, in case the mission went sideways. It wouldn't be used to defend her, it could be used to hurt her.

"So that's it then," she said.

"That's it."

What he didn't say, but they both knew, was that they could kill Cruz immediately once Alex was handed over.

And she would witness the entire thing.

23

Before Cruz descended from the blue Jeep, his gaze met Alissa's. Today her hair was in cornrows and she wore a black long-sleeved shirt under a bullet-proof vest.

She'd parked the vehicle facing away from the building. As soon as she had Alex strapped in, her job was to get the hell out of there. She nodded at him, confirming without words that she was ready to carry her precious cargo.

They both descended from the vehicle and walked slowly toward the men.

He counted seven total. Two on the roof carried AR-15s, there were two others on either side of the metal door at the front of the building, and three others waiting for him. Others would be inside.

They weren't all armed, but they did all wear Kevlar body armor and heavy boots, looking like they were ready for war. The one in the front, who seemed like the leader because he was positioned in front of the others, stood with both feet shoulder-width apart. His dark hair was cut low, military-style, and he had thick eyebrows over a protruding forehead.

"Not her! Just you," he said. "Get back."

Cruz recognized his voice. He was the person who'd called and given the coordinates—and refused to let him talk to his son.

He turned around to Alissa and nodded, and she went back to the vehicle. He then proceeded, stifling his rage by flexing the fingers of one hand.

The man in front eyed Cruz with a neutral expression as he approached. "Hello, Cruz. I'm Danny. I've heard a lot about you."

"Can't say the same," he returned.

Danny smirked. "Don't worry, you'll know a lot more about me very soon. You'll know way more than you ever wanted to."

Cruz stopped before him. "Where's my son?"

"Let's not get ahead of ourselves. Check him." Danny snapped his fingers and one of the other men, also with a buzz cut but blond, came forward.

Cruz lifted his arms and let the man pat him down, his gaze never dropping from Danny.

"He's clean," the blond said, then he went back into position.

"Good. You know how to follow directions." Danny looked back over his shoulder. "Get the kid."

One of the men escorted Alex out, holding his hand, and a little bit of tension left Cruz's body. Alex was wearing a purple Elmo T-shirt and yellow shorts. He looked unharmed and exactly the same as the last time he'd seen him—except that his lips and cheeks at the corners of his mouth were stained red.

As soon as Alex saw him, his eyes brightened.

"Daddy!" The man let him tug away, and Alex came barreling toward Cruz.

Cruz swept him up into his arms and clutched him tight. Relief. Bone-melting, consuming relief filled every crevice of his body as he squeezed his son into his chest. His heart felt as if it were about to burst out of his ribs, and if he didn't have an audience he might have crumbled to the ground.

"Are you okay?" he asked. He didn't want to alarm the boy, but he needed the reassurance.

Alex nodded and clung to his neck. "I was scared. I missed you and Mommy."

"We missed you, too." Cruz clutched Alex's head and kissed one of his plump cheeks. "Looks like you had some candy." He could smell the syrupy sweet.

Alex nodded. "Cherry lollipop. Don't tell Mommy," he added in a stage whisper.

Cruz laughed and kissed his son's forehead, more tension draining from his body. "I won't."

"We didn't hurt him," Danny said. "We're only interested in you."

Cruz's gaze flicked to his enemy as he imagined the many ways he could kill him.

"Can we go home now?" Alex asked, eyes round and pleading.

Cruz's voice was gentle when he spoke to his son. "You're going home, but I can't go yet. I need to stay here and talk to these men, okay?"

"No, Daddy. That man is a bad man. He won't give me Mr. Cuddles." Alex pouted and pointed his little finger at Danny.

Cruz's neck tightened with fury, but he kept his voice calm when he asked Danny, "Do you know where his stuffed alligator is?"

"No, I don't know where the fuck that is. What do I look like?" The men near him laughed.

"Watch your mouth around my kid," Cruz said.

Danny arched an eyebrow, as if he couldn't believe Cruz's audacity. "Pardon my language. I don't know where the toy is."

Cruz's jaw hardened as he locked eyes with Danny. "Where is he?" he asked Alex.

"I don't know." Anxiety seeped into his son's voice and tears pooled in his eyes. "Mommy's gonna be mad. She told me to take better care of Mr. Cuddles. I'm sorry."

"Hey, don't cry." Cruz tilted up his son's chin. "Mommy won't be mad, and I'll get Mr. Cuddles for you, okay?"

Alex sniffled and rubbed the tears from his eyes with his fists. "Promise?"

"I promise."

"Can we wrap this up?" Danny asked in an exasperated voice.

Cruz ignored him and planted kisses on each of Alex's cheeks, letting his lips linger for a longer period, taking in his little boy smell mixed with the scent of cherry lollipop.

"Is it all right if I take him to her?" he asked Danny.

"He can walk," Danny said, crossing his arms over his chest.

Cruz stared at him in heated silence. Yeah, he was going to enjoy bashing his head in. For now, he needed to keep calm so his son could get out of there safely. He set Alex on his feet and pointed at Alissa, who stood at the back of the Jeep. "See that woman over there?" Alissa waved at Alex. "Her name is Miss Alissa. She's going to take you to Mommy, okay?"

Alex's eyes lit up. "Mommy's here?"

"Yes."

"All right, *amigo*, let's go." Danny unholstered his gun but kept it pointed at the ground.

"Not in front of my son," Cruz bit out.

Alex must have sensed the tension, because he wrapped his little arms around Cruz's thigh and peered up at him. "Daddy?"

Cruz placed a comforting hand on his head. "It's okay, *mijo*. I'll see you later." He bent and kissed him again to ease his worry. "*Te quiero*. Go to Miss Alissa, and she'll take you to Mommy."

Alex stepped slowly toward Alissa, his little legs unsure.

Halfway there, he stopped and looked back, his brow wrinkled with uncertainty.

Cruz smiled to reassure him. "Go," he said, with a wave of his hand.

That seemed to be enough, and Alex continued walking. Alissa took a few steps forward and lifted him into her arms. Alex waved at Cruz over her shoulder, and Cruz waved back. Alex's frowning stare signaled he knew something was wrong and didn't understand what was going on. He knew his father should be coming with him.

Alissa placed him in the car seat and then hopped into the front. She started the Jeep and drove away. Cruz had instructed the crew to make sure Alex and Alissa were clear before the assault began.

But Cruz was still watching the Jeep carrying his son when his head exploded with pain, seeming to crack open with the force of a blunt blow. He tasted metal, and all the sound in the vicinity disappeared. He fought the blackness that threatened to overtake him, but the world around him went dark…before he fell to the dirt like a log.

24

Shanice watched in horror as one of the men dragged Cruz's limp body across the dirt. She was hiding in the woods on her stomach, looking down at the clearing through a tangle of leaves and brush. When Cruz had dropped, Alissa had increased her speed to get away. Her son might be safe, but Cruz had taken a vicious blow to the head.

"Do something!" she whispered fiercely to Kinsey, who was lying on her stomach with her sniper rifle and other gear beside her. The rest of the team was spread out in the woods.

The younger woman shook her head. "We can't. He told us not to."

"What?" Shanice watched as the men hauled Cruz through the door. "Are you saying he planned this?"

"Not planned, but he suspected it would happen." Kinsey cocked her head to the left and listened to whomever was speaking to her via the piece in her ear. "Okay," she said, nodding.

She sat up and dug into the outer pocket of the green, military-style shoulder sling next to her. She removed something and then extended her hand to Shanice. "Raheem wants you to clip this to your ear so you can hear what's going on. You'll also be able to communicate. Tap right there to turn it off and on."

Shanice attached the earpiece to the shell of her ear. Once it was securely fastened, she tentatively said, "Hello?"

"Hey, Shanice, this is Raheem. Cruz didn't want us trying to do anything until Alex was in the clear. If we tried to rescue Cruz, the gunmen on the roof might have shot at the Jeep to keep them from leaving—or worse. We're all professionals and good at what we do, but he didn't want us taking a single chance that Alex could get hurt."

Shanice closed her eyes. Grateful for his forethought but worried about his safety.

"Okay," she said through a tight throat.

"Don't worry, Cruz knows what he's doing."

Cruz was good at his job, but it was impossible not to worry when you loved someone as fiercely as she loved him.

"You ready to see your son?" Raheem asked.

"Yes."

"Bo, take her to Alissa," Raheem said.

One of the mercenaries—a bulky Black man named Bo with a medium-brown complexion—moved so quietly, she was surprised when he appeared behind her. He carried an unholstered gun in one hand.

He helped her to her feet.

Shanice removed the earpiece and tucked it into her pocket. "Goodbye, Kinsey," Shanice said.

"Goodbye." Kinsey remained focused on the building below them.

Shanice moved as quietly as she could between the trees for the almost one-mile trek. Bo didn't speak as he led the way, and that was fine with her. She tried to stay focused on the fact that Alex was safe and she was about to see him but couldn't shake the image of Cruz being knocked to the ground. Fear lodged in her throat, and she blinked back tears.

"Keep it together," she muttered to herself. Cruz would get out of this situation. She'd seen him in action before, she knew—

Shanice let out a small cry when a man dropped from a tree onto Bo, knocking him to the ground. His gun tumbled from his hand, and he and the attacker started struggling.

The other man was gigantic, taller than Bo and his long body was lined with muscles. He and Bo rolled on the ground as each tried to get the upper hand. Bo managed to toss him off, but the other man quickly knocked him to the ground with a snarl and jumped on top of him. He plunged a knife toward Bo's face, but Bo blocked the death blow and gritted his teeth as the man pressed down toward his eye.

"Get the gun!" Bo gasped, his voice coming out tight as he struggled to breathe under the weight of the man on top of him.

Shanice scrambled into action and found the weapon tucked under a small bush. She pointed it at the attacker and said, "Stop, or I'll shoot."

Why did she sound so weak? Her voice shook. Her hands shook. He paid her no mind.

"Shoot him!" Bo choked out the words.

She swallowed back the ball of fear in her throat. Could she really shoot someone? Could she shoot without hitting Bo? This was why Cruz had told her she should practice more regularly. Why hadn't she listened to him?

"Shoot him!" Bo begged. The knife was less than an inch from his eye.

Shanice heard Cruz's voice in her head. *Don't forget your shooting stance. You want a sturdy base.* She positioned her feet shoulder-width apart.

Line up your sights. She focused on the front sight of the gun, aiming at the man on top of Bo.

Take your time when you squeeze the trigger. Nice and easy. She squeezed the trigger and the bullet missed. She jumped, startled by the loud noise the gun made.

"Come on, Shanice, you can do this," she whispered.

She held her hand steady and squeezed again. The man's head jerked to the left and he fell over onto his side.

Shanice gasped and dropped the gun. Body tight with tension, she stared at the unmoving body.

Bo sat up, panting and wiping blood spatter off his cheek and forehead. He looked at the dead man and then looked at her. "Are you okay?" His breath came in long heaves.

"No," Shanice answered in a shaky, husky voice. She'd killed someone. She'd actually *killed* someone.

Hunter broke through the trees at full speed, handgun drawn, but skidded to a halt when he saw them. He assessed the scene, his gaze landing on the discarded gun at Shanice's feet. "Are you all right?"

She lifted her eyes to his and saw the depth of his concern. Straightening her shoulders, she said, "I will be. I need to see my son."

Hunter placed a hand to his ear. "They're fine." He tapped the earpiece again and said to Bo, "I'll take care of this guy. Get her out of here."

Bo rushed to his feet and picked up his gun. He placed a gentle hand on Shanice's arm. "Come on," he said softly.

She walked beside him on shaky knees, refusing to look back at the man on the ground.

Before too long, they came to the roadway. Alissa had parked on the shoulder and was waiting inside with Alex. The minute Shanice saw her son's face peeking out the window in the back seat, she took off into a run.

When he saw her, his face broke into a grin. Shanice yanked open the door and climbed onto the seat. "Hey, sweet pea." Her voice cracked.

"Hi, Mommy!" Alex exclaimed.

She took him from the seat and into a fierce hug. "Are you okay?"

Alex nodded.

She fought the urge to cry because she didn't want to upset him, but failed miserably. Tears rolled down her cheeks and she angrily wiped them away.

"Why are you crying, Mommy? Are you sad?" Alex asked anxiously.

"No, sweet pea, these are happy tears," Shanice choked out in a thick voice. "I'm so happy to see you. I missed you."

"I missed you, too."

Shanice hugged Alex again. Then she scanned him, looking for injury or a sign that he'd been mistreated in any way. He was wearing the same clothes from yesterday, and his shirt was wrinkled but he seemed fine. All she saw was his bright smile and red lips, as if he'd eaten candy. She showered kisses on his plump cheeks and eyes and nose. Alex laughed at the attention and then returned the kisses. He was so pure and innocent. Maybe he had no idea the danger he'd been in. Maybe none of this would matter later and mentally, he'd be fine, unaffected by the ordeal. She'd have him talk to a therapist to make sure.

Shanice squeezed him tight. "I love you so much."

"I love you, too, Mommy," he said, arms wrapped around her neck.

It took a while, but Shanice finally felt comfortable enough to release him and set him back in the car seat. Alissa was standing on the outside of the Jeep, talking to Bo a few feet away, giving her the private moments with her son.

"Alissa."

She turned.

"I'm ready."

"Later," Alissa said to Bo, with her Caribbean accent. Shanice could listen to her read the ingredients on a bag of chips.

Bo saluted and Shanice waved goodbye. She closed the door and strapped in beside Alex. Alissa was taking them to a clinic where Miriam waited. The Cordoba Agency had made arrangements with the facility to ensure confidentiality, and a doctor would check Alex for injury and trauma, but she doubted they'd find any. He seemed surprisingly well-adjusted. No doubt the candy helped, but she had to assume that they hadn't been cruel to her son. Thankfully.

On the way to the clinic, Alex chatted away like normal, and she forced a smile to her lips while her stomach was in knots. He even told her that his daddy said he would get Mr. Cuddles, and he seemed confident that would happen. His daddy had promised, after all.

But Shanice knew the last thing on Cruz's mind was that dang alligator. She kept thinking about how they'd dragged his limp body into that building. She knew they wouldn't treat her husband with the same care they'd treated her son. She didn't even know if he'd come out alive because the whole point of this meeting was to exchange his life for Alex's.

Shanice turned away from her son so he wouldn't see her face crumble under the weight of worry. Gnawing on her bottom lip, she pushed back against the negative thoughts.

Cruz was a warrior and knew what he was doing. He would make it out alive.

He had to.

25

Cruz awoke to the sound of male voices talking and laughing. He came to slowly, disoriented, head throbbing and body filled with aches and pains. A few seconds passed before he remembered what happened, but the tinny scent of blood brought back the memory of the blow to the back of his head. He could feel how the thick liquid had dried on his neck.

He tried to move and realized that his movements were limited. His feet rested on a cool surface, and he could move his legs but had limited mobility in his arms.

"He's waking up," one of the men said.

"Finally." That was Danny.

Groggy and disoriented, Cruz opened his eyes and slowly lifted his gaze. With that slight movement, his head throbbed more. The lack of natural light and enclosed atmosphere of the room suggested they were underground.

"Hey, you awake now?" The question came from in front but below him. The blond tapped Cruz's thigh with a baton.

Cruz was temporarily confused. How was the man *below*

him? Then understanding dawned. The ache in his arms, the inability to move, all indicated what they'd done.

Cruz was naked except for his blue boxer briefs, and that cool surface was a square-shaped metal table. He lifted his head and saw his arms were stretched above him. He saw a single length of rope was wrapped around each wrist, and that rope was wound around a bar—a sturdy piece of horizontal wood attached to thick wedges that were bolted to the low ceiling. He suspected they'd constructed the contraption just for him.

There were three men in the room. The blond from outside was the closest, then there was another guy seated on a wood chair with his arms crossed and his ankle settled on one knee. He was dark-haired like Danny and had thick eyebrows. Danny leaned against the back wall, looking at Cruz with amusement in his dark eyes. The *cabrón* was damn near gleeful at the predicament Cruz was in.

"Hey, answer me." Blondie whacked Cruz's thigh with the baton, and pain shot up his leg.

Goddamn. Cruz grunted and listened to them laugh. The way his body hurt, they must have beat him while he was unconscious.

"I saw your file." That was Danny. "You're supposed to be a real tough guy, but we got you easy enough. What do you think about that?"

Cruz didn't answer, rotating his neck to work out the kinks and pushing through the pain to scan the room. There was only one door—a metal one in the middle of the wall to his right. Danny had a Beretta in a holster at his waist and seemed to be the only one carrying a firearm. The blond didn't have any visible weapons besides the baton but could very well be armed with a knife or a smaller gun clipped to his ankle. Lean but muscular, the brunette seemed armed only with a dumb expression on his face.

"Danny's talking to you. Answer him!"

Blondie struck him again, harder this time, and Cruz let out an agonized groan, gritting his teeth against the blistering pain that burst on his flesh.

"You ain't so tough, are you? I'm looking forward to putting a bullet in your eye." Danny held up one hand as if he were looking through the scope of a rifle and pretended to fire into Cruz's face, adding sound effects with his mouth.

"What's stopping you?" Cruz croaked. His mouth was dry and tasted stale, and his tongue felt heavy, all signs that he'd been unconscious for at least a couple of hours.

"He speaks!" Danny threw up his hands like someone cheering at a football game after a touchdown.

The other two men laughed and mockingly clapped their hands.

"Logan wants to watch you die. We're just waiting for his call." Danny patted the phone clipped to his hip.

Cruz had guessed as much based on his conversation with Logan. The old guy wanted to watch them murder him.

"Guess that's what happens when you fuck with someone's family," Blondie said.

"Where's my son's stuffed animal?" Cruz scanned the room in a fruitless hope that Mr. Cuddles was in there.

"Frankly, you've got bigger issues to worry about than a stupid toy," Danny said. "We got you, Cordoba. You were too easy to grab. I thought for sure you'd put up a fight."

"Maybe I planned it this way so I could destroy you from the inside. Where's the stuffed alligator? I promised my son I'd get it back for him."

Danny smirked. "Forget the toy. Do you understand where you are and the predicament you're in? You expect me to believe this is all part of your master plan? Us grabbing you, beating the shit out of you, and hanging you from the ceiling like a piece of meat? When I shoot you in the face, that's part of the plan, too, I guess? I gotta tell you, man, your plan sucks. I'm not impressed."

"Maybe you're a dumbass and don't know what's about to hit you."

Danny pushed away from the wall. "Oh, *I'm* the dumbass? Where's your crew? You got one of my men in the woods, but when we get done with you, our whole team is going out there, and we're going to find and slaughter every one of them."

"Never gonna happen."

Danny laughed again, shaking his head. "You're mighty confident for a man whose crew let him get captured. They haven't even tried to come in."

"They're waiting on my signal."

"Your signal? You're tied to a ceiling in our basement. We stripped you down to your skivvies and we're going to kill you. What signal can you give, asshole?"

"You'll see, dumbass."

"Stop calling me that!" Danny yelled.

Cruz laughed long and hard to piss him off, stretching his neck and loosening his muscles in anticipation of his next steps.

"Too bad we didn't have more time to have some fun with him," the blond said.

"We can't have fun with him, but we can have some fun with his family. Hey, Cordoba, when you're gone, I think I'll fuck your wife and have your son call me daddy. Or is that *papi*?"

Danny stared him in the eyes while the other two laughed.

Cruz glared at Danny, fury billowing in his blood. "Don't talk about my family."

Danny took a couple of steps closer. "What did you say?"

"I *said*, don't talk about my family."

"Fuck. You." Using his foot, Danny shoved the table from under Cruz's feet, and he dropped into dead air.

He uttered a groan of pain as the rope cut into his wrists, further bruising his flesh as they supported all his weight. The wrists were not meant to hold the weight of the entire body, which meant he had to move quickly before he lost feeling in his arms. Even worse, he could dislocate his shoulders and pass out.

Danny turned away from him in disgust, walking toward the back of the room. Mapping a course of action based on the positions of the men in the room, Cruz gripped the ropes to ease the pull on his arms. "No, fuck *you*."

He swung his long body forward and kicked Blondie in the face. With a yelp, the man staggered back, but Cruz didn't waste time watching where he landed. With a surge of energy, he shot his body up to the wooden bar and pulled himself higher. Curling his body up, he kicked the corner of the bar twice with the heel of his foot. The bar splintered on the first kick and broke on the second. Cruz dropped to his feet on the cement floor.

The dark-haired man growled and charged at him, but Cruz flipped backward over the table, grabbed two of the legs and raced toward him and the blond. He used the table like a battering ram and slammed the brunette into the blond. As the brunette fell, Cruz followed up with a blow to the blond, knocking him into the wall, and he fell to the floor, unconscious.

"You son of a..." the brunette muttered. He was on his feet and trying to circle around Cruz.

"Get him!" Danny yelled, pulling the Beretta.

Cruz tossed the table at him as he fired off a shot that ricocheted against the metal surface, and then he kicked the brunette in the chest. His opponent shuffled backward but didn't fall. He was stronger than he looked. Cruz followed by running up onto the chair. He used it as a launchpad, clasping his hands together and bringing them down like a club on the other man's temple—sure to rattle his brain in his skull. He toppled to the ground and his head hit the cement floor with a loud crack.

Cruz hauled up the semi-conscious man as Danny swung the gun at him and fired a round. The bullet hit the brunette's Kevlar vest and Cruz kept going, using the other man as a shield. In a shameful display of panic, Danny kept firing in quick succession, the bullets slamming into his partner's chest and forcing constant moans from his lips as his body convulsed from the hammerlike power of each projectile.

Cruz kept low behind the brunette, but eyed Danny, whose back was plastered against the wall, arms extended in a firm shooting grip. Within several feet, he tossed the brunette at Danny, who did what he expected him to—he dodged out of the way.

Before he had time to recover, Cruz rushed him and they struggled for a few seconds before the gun dislodged from his hand and toppled to the ground out of reach. They both stared, sizing each other up. Then Cruz smirked at Danny, and that set him off.

With a frustrated growl, Danny rushed toward him. He swung his fist, which Cruz dodged, and with a smooth twist and turn Cruz wrapped Danny's wrist in the rope that still bound his own hands together. Danny swung with his left hand, but Cruz shifted and the blow only grazed his ear. He then swiped Danny's feet from under him and with rapid movements, unwound the rope from his wrist and twisted it around his neck.

Danny gasped as his oxygen was cut off, and reached back. Cruz remained bending over him but stretched his neck and torso back, moving out of reach so he couldn't gouge his eyes.

"What was that you said about my wife and kid?" Cruz said between gritted teeth. He yanked the rope and Danny's feet kicked out in panic as he clawed at his neck in a fight for air.

The sound of Danny's phone ringing filled the room with a shrill cry. Cruz didn't have to look at the screen to know the call was probably *Private*. Nor did he have to answer to know that Randall Logan was on the other end of the line.

Sensing a shift in the air behind him, Cruz turned. The blond was awake, and his arm came swinging toward Cruz. He caught the flash of a short blade and moved to the side, but not fast enough. The knife was meant to go into his neck, but instead white-hot pain sliced through his left shoulder blade.

His muscles screamed, and he dropped to one knee, but as quickly as the agony came, he shoved it aside. He'd been trained since the age of eighteen to push his body to the limits of endurance and push past his pain threshold to perform his duty. This moment would be no different.

Cruz rotated his core and came up with a vicious elbow strike that landed in the middle of Blondie's face. The man yelped and blood gushed from his broken nose. Cruz hadn't released Danny, and his movement yanked the rope and Danny's body with it.

Cruz followed up with a back kick that sent the blond careening backward. He crashed onto his back, stunned. With nothing but brute strength and determination, Cruz dragged Danny's struggling body with him over to the blond and stomped his throat with the heel of his foot. The man spasmed, eyes rolling back in his head as his windpipe was destroyed. Cruz stomped his throat again, and this time only a faint gurgling sound was heard before his body went limp.

Cruz pushed Danny onto his stomach and pressed his knee into his back, forcing him to struggle even more for air. Not wanting any more surprises, he glanced at the brunette's supine body to ensure he was still out cold, when the phone at Danny's hip started ringing again. That would be Logan calling back for his viewing party. He would know something was wrong when the phone went unanswered again, and he'd reach out to other members of The Custer Brigade. Cruz had to move fast.

He yanked the rope tighter and watched as Danny's face turned ruby-red and a vein popped in his forehead. He was in panic mode now and knew he was going to die. His hands alternated between flailing and pointlessly clutching at the rope.

Cruz didn't let up, muscles tightening under the exertion. He remained emotionless and resolute in the face of his enemy's suffering.

Finally, Danny's hands fell away and his body ceased moving. Cruz held his position for ten seconds longer to make sure. Then he unwound the rope and let Danny's head drop to the floor.

Chest heaving, he stood over his vanquished adversary. "You impressed now, motherfucker?"

Cruz picked up the gun from the corner and shot all three men in the head. Not out of some gruesome sense of overkill, but out of an abundance of caution. He knew better than to leave anything to chance. More men would be coming soon, and he couldn't risk one of them rising up and attacking him as he secured the room.

He checked the magazine in the Beretta. He had three rounds left and didn't want to waste a single one shooting off the rope around his wrists. He could fight just fine with this handicap. He wished he could provide a little protection for himself by putting on one of their vests, but he still had the knife sticking out of his back. He could feel the trickle of blood down his back, and it hurt like hell. But he couldn't remove the blade and risk causing more damage, which included the potential to bleed out because he had no way to take care of the wound.

His ears picked up movement outside the door. Moving quickly, he turned out the light and crouched against the wall in the dark. The door was in the middle of the room, and if the men moved like he would, they'd have men on each side and enter swiftly, one at a time to clear the room. But he had darkness on his side.

In the quiet, his trained ears heard them edge closer, and then he saw the shadows beneath the door. He lifted the handgun higher, aiming for above the vest.

The door burst open and he fired two shots, shooting the first man in the neck, his vulnerable spot between the helmet and his bulletproof vest. He collapsed into the room on his face, never getting off a single round. A second man had ducked out as soon as he heard the gunfire, and the others behind him fell back. A quick glance let Cruz see there were at least six more men out there—a manageable number.

He dragged the dead man all the way into the room and the door slid closed. He only had seconds before they came at him again. He flicked on the light and took the dead man's AR-15 and searched him for other weapons. Finding a knife in an ankle holster, he used it to cut off the ropes around his wrists. Then he strapped the holster and knife to his right ankle.

He tucked the Beretta into the waistband of his boxer briefs at his side and stood. He turned off the light, and with the AR-15 clasped in his hands, he now felt battle ready.

This time, he crouched on the other side of the door, and almost immediately it was tossed open from the other side.

Let the games begin.

26

There were three men on the roof now.

Shanice had returned to her spot beside Kinsey to see about Cruz. Lights lit up the two-story structure and the surrounding grounds, but all around was dark, with night critters serenading them in the bushes.

After an examination by a doctor at the clinic confirmed Alex was fine, Shanice had been relieved. She gave him a bath and nourishing meal, and he fell fast asleep in the big bed in the hotel suite Cruz had booked for them. Shanice lay down beside her son and watched him sleep, but nonstop thoughts about Cruz made her realize she had to go back or she'd go crazy.

She told one of the bodyguards she wanted to return to the site. Arrangements were made and she hugged her mother goodbye, whose worried face displayed her concern at her decision to go back. But Shanice felt she had no choice. How could she stay there in the plush comfort of the hotel suite while Cruz was held prisoner and forced to endure whatever evil those men conjured to hurt him? The simple answer was, she couldn't. Assured her mother and Alex were safe at the hotel with the men watching over them, she was more than willing to take the risk and go back.

Gunfire erupted from inside the building, and Shanice held her breath. That had to be good, right? Cruz was probably fighting, because those men wouldn't shoot at each other.

Unless...they were shooting at *him*.

No, don't think like that, she chided herself, uttering a quick, pleading prayer for his safety.

The men on the roof moved around agitatedly, and one of them held a hand to his ear, possibly talking to someone inside the building. At the same time one of the windows on the top floor drew Shanice's attention because a light flashed on and off inside.

"There it is!" Raheem's voice burst excitedly through the earpiece. "That's our signal."

"Is it Cruz? How do you know?" Shanice asked.

"It's S.O.S. in Morse code," Raheem replied.

Kinsey got in position and adjusted her scope. She'd hardly moved for hours. The level of discipline displayed by her and the others was admirable.

"You ready, Mouse?" Raheem asked.

"You bet I am," the young woman said, pressing her cheek against the weapon. Even in the dark, Shanice saw how her features settled into lines of deep concentration.

"Do your thing, baby."

In quick succession, she shot two of the men on the roof. The last one, after watching his partners fall, took off running and fired his weapon in Kinsey and Shanice's general direction. Bullets spewed from the muzzle as he swung the gun in a wide arch, but they landed without damage because they were too far away.

The man dived behind an air conditioning unit, but the second he eased his head above the large barrier, Kinsey pulled the trigger a third time and clipped the top of his head. He collapsed onto his back, dead.

"Go!" Raheem yelled.

Five men, dressed in black tactical gear that included body armor and helmets with clear bullet-proof face shields, ran out of the trees. Weapons in hand, they advanced toward the building in a methodical fashion. As they neared the building they fanned out—three to the front and two to the back.

Shanice watched in awe as the ones in the front set up explosives on the door and stood back. A loud blast blew off the metal door and smoke billowed at the entry point. The group of three rushed in, and seconds later, there was another loud blast at the back of the building. She imagined them rushing in, too.

The sound of gunfire filled the night air. Crouched low and biting the knuckles of her left hand, Shanice kept her eyes on the scene before her, wishing she could see the action unfold but equally concerned that she might not be able to sleep if she did. She wanted everyone to come out safe, but especially Cruz.

A man came tearing from the back of the building. He didn't have a gun, and his legs and arms pumped fast as he moved with great speed toward the path leading into the trees. The muzzle of Kinsey's sniper rifle followed him for a few seconds before she pulled the trigger, knocking his dead body to the dirt as easily as swatting a fly.

The next few minutes were tense with the occasional sound of shots fired, and from that distance, Shanice also heard yelling, though she couldn't tell what anyone was saying. Still no sign of Cruz, but she was hopeful. If he'd managed to get a message to them, he had to be alive.

While Kinsey remained in position, Shanice rose to her feet. She couldn't stay still anymore. She needed to get rid of her nervous energy.

"We're on our way back," she heard Hunter say.

Two members of the team burst out of the entrance. She

recognized him in the front, running with a bag thrown over his shoulder.

Two more team members ran out behind them. Not too long after, another man exited, and she recognized him as Sanchez.

She held her breath, eyes searching frantically for Cruz. Where was he?

"Where's Cruz?" Raheem asked.

"He told us to set the explosives and get out. He had to go back for something," Hunter said.

"What the fuck? What the hell did he have to go back for?" Raheem demanded.

"I don't know. He didn't say. He told us to get out and told Sanchez to start the countdown. He said he'd get out in time."

"And you motherfuckers left him in there?" Raheem demanded.

"He told us to!" Hunter said.

Raheem uttered a stream of curses and then apparently removed his device because Shanice could no longer hear him clearly—only muffled sounds of discontent.

Why would he go back? her panicked brain demanded.

"Crap," Kinsey said quietly, keeping her eyes on the building.

Shanice tapped her earpiece to turn off the microphone. "Do you know why he went back? What could he have forgotten?" she asked.

Kinsey shook her head, focused on the scene before her. "I don't know."

"How much time do we have before the explosives go off?"

When she saw Kinsey's doleful expression, her heart plummeted.

"Less than two minutes," the younger woman said quietly.

Shanice fell to her knees beside Kinsey. "He'll get out in time," she said to herself.

"Yes, he will. I was once in a crazy situation with Cruz and he got me and him out of there." Kinsey laughed softly at the memory. "I owe him my life. He's gonna get out. Failure's not an option for your husband." She spared a glance at Shanice and smiled reassuringly.

Shanice nodded her agreement and turned her attention to the scene before them. *Come on, Cruz.*

"Come on, Cruz," Raheem muttered into the earpiece, echoing her thoughts. "Where are you, brother?"

Time ticked by, and without a watch, Shanice couldn't keep track, but those two minutes had to be the longest in history.

He's gonna get out, she told herself. And when he did, she was going to beat the crap out of him for scaring her so bad—

Boom!

Shanice flinched and cowered to the ground. The building had exploded and rocked the area. The air shook. Smoke billowed toward the black sky and sparks shot into the surrounding trees, setting leaves on fire, knocking out some of the lights and scattering debris all over the property. Slowly straightening on her knees, Shanice's mouth fell open as she stared at the destroyed structure.

"Holy shit," a male voice muttered.

She didn't know if that was Hunter or Raheem.

Then there was nothing but silence. No one spoke a word, as if the entire team was holding its breath.

No. No. No. Babe, please come back to me. You promised.

Her eyes frantically scoured the carnage below. He had to have made his way out. She didn't know what she would do without him. After more than three years together, Cruz was her everything, the man she had been put on this earth to love.

The scent of smoke and ash burned the air. Breathing was difficult, with her breaths coming in slow, uneven spurts and eyes sweeping the burning building. Nothing could have survived that blast.

The minutes dragged by as black smoke and flames reached for the sky.

Baby, where are you? Tears blurred her vision, but Shanice willed herself not to cry. *Come on. Come on...*

"There! To the left!" Raheem yelled.

Shanice scrambled to the edge of their hiding place on all fours, swinging her eyes in the direction Raheem indicated, searching for the evidence he saw.

"Alissa, Hunter, Bo, go! Go!" Raheem bellowed.

Shanice caught movement at the left corner of what was left of the crumbled building.

"There he is!" she screamed, as if they hadn't already seen him.

Her beloved husband, her hero, crawled away from the flames and then struggled to his feet. She could barely see him because there wasn't as much light as before and he was covered in black soot and naked except for his boxer briefs.

"Oh, god. Baby..." Shanice whispered. Tears spilled onto her cheeks, and her heart grieved at what he must have endured.

As he came closer, she saw he clutched something—an object was crushed against his chest with one arm. Was that... was that *Mr. Cuddles*?

He staggered and collapsed onto his stomach.

"Cruz!"

Shanice almost jumped to her feet, but Kinsey placed a restraining hand on her arm.

"They'll get him," she promised.

The words had no sooner left her mouth than the same blue Jeep that had carried her and Alex away, sped onto the scene. Shanice craned her neck, watching as Hunter and Bo hopped out and lifted Cruz under the arms, his head hanging loosely between his shoulders. The stuffed animal dropped into the dirt as the men hauled his big body into the back seat.

Before they pulled him in, Shanice noticed an object

sticking out of his back. "Oh my goodness," she whispered. What had they done to him?

Hunter ran back to pick up the toy and then climbed into the back seat. Alissa shoved the transmission into gear and they sped away, back up the hillside and into the trees.

Kinsey started packing up her gear.

Shanice turned on the mic. "Where are they taking him, Raheem?" she asked.

"To the same clinic where they took Alex," Raheem answered. "Simmons and Sanchez are coming to get you, ladies. I'll meet you roadside."

Kinsey slung her bag over her shoulder. "Let's go."

27

Cruz groaned as he slowly awoke in the hospital bed, and Shanice tightened her hand around his. Not too much, though, because she was afraid of hurting him. She simply wanted him to know she was there.

His eyes fluttered open and gradually focused on her face.

"Hey," she said softly, smiling at him from her seat beside the bed.

When she first arrived at the clinic, she'd burst into tears when she saw him up close—tousled hair, bleeding, and covered in soot. She'd been there since he arrived last night and hadn't left his side except when he'd gone through minor surgery to remove the knife in his back. He'd been in and out of consciousness, at one point whispering her name before falling into oblivion.

They smiled at each other now.

"You gave me quite a scare," Shanice said.

"Didn't mean to." His voice sounded dry.

"Are you thirsty?"

"A little."

She poured water in a plastic cup and held it to his mouth.

He sat up enough to drink it all before replacing his head on the pillow.

"How do you feel?"

"Not too bad, considering."

"Well, you're high on morphine right now."

He laughed softly. "My old friend morphine comes through again."

He was surprisingly light-hearted considering what he'd been through, but he was used to these adventures in his previous line of work. The trauma and stress was all outside of the norm for her. She still couldn't fully comprehend what he'd done—putting himself in harm's way, exchanging his life for Alex's to ensure their son's safety, and take down all those men.

Inside the facility he'd been beaten—evidenced by the bruising on his body and the need for him to lie with his head elevated because of bruised ribs. He'd been stabbed in the back and apparently had barely escaped the building before it exploded. The blast had thrown him several feet and covered him in soot. How he managed to get up and walk into view so they would know he was alive had taken a tremendous amount of strength—probably the last he had, which was why he'd collapsed and ended up more or less knocked out for the past twelve hours.

"I can't believe you went back to get Mr. Cuddles. What were you thinking?" She was still angry about his insane decision. If he wasn't broken up and in the hospital bed, she'd hit him. "We could have bought him another one."

Cruz shook his head. "Not the same. He would have known. That one has an eye missing, and a new one would have been too obviously...new."

"You could have died."

"I promised him I'd get it."

"So what? You risked your life—"

"I will *not* break my promises to him." His voice was firm and his eyes flashed angrily at her for a split second.

Shanice fell silent. He hardly ever raised his voice at her, so when he did, she knew to pay attention because that meant he wasn't putting up with her crap. She took his hand to convey she'd abandon chastising his decision. Alex had Mr. Cuddles, and Cruz was safe. That was all that mattered.

His fingers closed around her hand. "How's our boy?"

"He's fine. Right now he's with my mom and Raheem, Bo, and Hunter at the hotel. Raheem wanted me to tell you that you didn't lose a single man or woman."

"Good. Doesn't always work out that way, but that's the way it should be."

"When they knocked you out and took you..." Shanice choked on the memory of her fear, her panic that they'd hurt him and she'd never see him alive again.

"That's one of the reasons I didn't want you there. I didn't want you to see anything like that. I know what men like that are capable of."

"There was no way you could have kept me away. I told you that."

"I know." He tugged her hand. "*Ven aca.* Get in the bed with me."

"I can't. You're hurt, and what will the doctor and nurses say when they come in?"

"Come. Here. I want to feel my wife next to me."

Shanice checked the door and then decided, *what the hell.* This was her man, her husband, and he wanted her close and she wanted to be close to him.

She eased onto the bed and carefully draped an arm across his middle. He took her hand in his.

"That feels better, doesn't it?" he asked, his deep voice rumbling in her ear.

"Mhmm," she agreed, settling against him. This was the best feeling in the world—being close to him, smelling him.

"Did Alex get Mr. Cuddles?"

"Yes. Mom washed him first."

"Was he happy?"

"Very. We talked via FaceTime, and he was very happy his daddy got Mr. Cuddles from the bad man." She paused. "How did you manage to keep fighting after they stabbed you?"

"I don't know how to explain, except to say it's instinctual after years of practice. Your body is powered by adrenaline and knows that if you stop, there will be consequences. So you don't stop until you're done."

"Or they kill you."

Cruz played with her fingers but didn't comment. "How does Alex seem to you?" he asked.

"He seems fine. I think he was confused at first, but they didn't hurt him. The doctors saw no signs of trauma or injury."

"Good."

She brushed his jaw with the back of her hand. "Babe, get some sleep, okay? Rest. I want you home sooner rather than later."

"You going to take care of me when they let me out of this place?"

She looked into his eyes, and though he was smiling, she kept her expression serious. "I'll gladly do whatever needs to be done. We made vows, remember? For richer, for poorer. In sickness and in health."

"You'll have to clean my wound and cater to me," Cruz said with a twinkle in his eye.

"I'm going to take such good care of you." Gazing into his eyes, she let her fingertips trail over his stubbled chin.

"Dame un beso," he whispered.

Shanice eased up and gently kissed his lips. She kissed his cheek and his neck, and he moaned.

"Sorry, baby."

When she tried to pull back, he grabbed her around the waist but winced with the effort.

"Cruz..."

"I'm fine. Come here."

She resettled against him and carefully placed her head on his shoulder. Her nipples pebbled and her loins immediately hummed with the desire to be closer and share greater intimacy, but now was not the time.

By the tent in the sheet, apparently his body had come alive, too.

"What's that?" Shanice teased.

"What?" Cruz asked innocently.

She giggled. "You're not that hurt, are you?"

He chuckled. "You could climb on and do all the work. I'll just lay here."

"Go to sleep." She kissed his jaw. "I love you."

"I love you, too, *mami*."

28

S hanice parked the car in the garage, and Cruz exited from the passenger side. She'd insisted on driving from the airport even though he told her he was fine. He finally let her have her way, realizing that she needed to do *something* for him. He still recalled the fear that gripped him when she'd been hauled out of the SUV by Logan's son in D.C., so he understood how helpless she'd felt watching him get hurt, and her worry about his recovery.

When they entered the living room, he saw Raheem typing on a computer on his lap. Alex huddled on the sofa with Miriam and Mr. Cuddles, reading a book. They had all returned a day earlier than Cruz and Shanice.

His heart suddenly became full. In Tennessee, Shanice had split her time between Cruz during the day and returning in the evening to be with Alex. According to what she'd told him, Alex had resorted back to sucking his thumb during the first few days, but gradually he'd returned to his normal self. They'd already scheduled an appointment with a child therapist to make sure there was no lasting emotional damage, but right now he looked as if nothing unusual had happened, and that's the way it should be.

The minute Alex saw his father, his eyes widened with joy, and he hopped off the sofa. "Daddy!"

He raced over and Cruz lifted him in his arms. He ignored the pain that remained from his healing ribs and the stab wound and indulged in the simple pleasure of giving his son a hug.

"I missed you," Alex said, clinging to Cruz's shoulders.

"I missed you, too."

"Grandma said you were sick."

"I was, and I had to stay with the doctor for a while so he could make me better."

"Are you better now?"

"I sure am." Cruz cupped the back of his head and kissed his cheek, once again relieved to have him home—safe, healthy, and away from harm.

When Cruz placed him on the floor, Miriam came over and gave him a brief hug. "Glad you're finally home," she whispered, patting his back.

Raheem stood nearby. "Good to have you back. You need me to stick around?"

"No, we're good. Thank you." Cruz gave him some dap and clapped his shoulder.

"Would you like to stay for dinner?" Shanice asked.

"No, I'm going to head back to my apartment and let you guys catch up." Raheem put away his laptop and retrieved his overnight bag from one of the guest rooms. "See you later, my man." He lowered his hand for a high-five to Alex.

"Bye, Raheem." Alex enthusiastically jumped and slapped his palm.

"I'll walk you out." Cruz picked up Raheem's computer bag and followed his friend out the front door to the brown Tahoe parked in the driveway.

Raheem opened the back door and tossed in his bag.

"Find anything that we can use?" Cruz asked, as he handed over the computer bag.

While in the hospital, he'd been in close contact with Raheem about the hard drives and other electronic data they'd taken from The Custer Brigade.

Raheem shook his head. "Nothing much that we could use, but I kept everything. You can take a look when you return to work. I turned over some of the intel to Miles like you asked, and he was appreciative. By the way, he wants you to give him a call when you get a chance."

Miles had gotten an assistant director post in Homeland Security, working in the Office for Targeted Violence and Terrorism Prevention.

"Okay. I guess that's it, then. Drive carefully. I'll see you tomorrow."

"You know good and well Shanice ain' letting you come back to work tomorrow." Raheem climbed into the SUV.

"We'll see," Cruz said with a laugh, though his friend was probably right.

Raheem backed down the driveway and Cruz went inside.

CRUZ WALKED through the quiet house, making sure all the doors and windows were locked. He rolled his neck and winced when his back throbbed. His bandaged wound ached, but not as much as when the blade had initially sliced through his flesh.

Miriam had prepared a delicious meal of roasted chicken, potatoes, and green beans. They'd also celebrated his return with a welcome home cake from Aunt Bessie's Sweets N Things Bakery. Alex had been very enthusiastic about the cake, getting icing all on his nose, cheeks, and hands before Miriam carted him off to the bathroom to get cleaned up.

Cruz peeked in on his son. Mr. Cuddles was on the floor, and Alex was sprawled in his Spider-man bed. His obsession with the superhero began after he watched *Spider-man: Into the Spider-Verse* with Cruz and Shanice one night. He didn't understand everything that had taken place, and he'd fallen asleep before the end of the movie, but ever since then he'd been in love with everything Spider-man related. His headboard and footboard had colorful images of Spider-man on them, and on the wall above his head was the framed comic-book character swinging into action from atop a building.

Cruz placed Mr. Cuddles next to Alex and tucked the sheet higher on his son's chest. He kissed his forehead and then quietly left the room.

Inside the master bedroom, only a lamp was on, and Shanice had placed his pajama pants across the foot of the bed.

She entered the bedroom from the bathroom carrying a glass of water and a little plastic cup filled with pills. "Pain killers and other medication the doctor said I should make sure you take," she said.

Cruz sighed.

"Cruz, don't be difficult. I know you're healthy and strong, but these will help and they are *prescribed* by a *doctor*. This is not me being overly cautious."

"I don't need any of that."

"Humor me," she said, extending her hand with the pills.

Cruz crossed his arms over his chest.

"If you don't take these, there will be no sex in this house for a very long time." Shanice arched an eyebrow.

He marched over and snatched the cup and glass from her hand. He tossed back the pills and chased them down his throat with the water.

Shanice doubled over in laughter. "Really, Cruz?"

"You threatened me with the worst punishment possible. What did you think I'd do?"

"You're so difficult." She placed the glass and cup on the table beside the bed. "I ran you a bath so you can relax, okay? Let me help you get undressed." She reached for his shirt.

He sighed. "Shanice, I don't need help getting undressed. I'm fine." She'd tried to help him get dressed at the hospital, but he'd brushed her away. He wasn't an invalid.

"Would you stop!" She slapped his chest, her voice cracking with emotion. She bit her bottom lip as if the outburst had taken her by surprise as much as it had him. "Let me help you. Please."

Cruz had been injured before, but nothing this bad in a while, and certainly not since they were married. In the most recent years pre-Hopevale, the most he'd experienced was a few bumps and bruises, minor injuries that he easily recovered from. But in Tennessee, he'd purposely put himself in harm's way to make sure his son was safe. The injuries and stay in the hospital were the worst he'd experienced in a long time, and for Shanice, it was all very traumatic. She wanted to take care of him, so he'd let her.

He tipped up her chin and looked down into her watery eyes. "Okay," he said softly.

Shanice sniffed and wiped her eyes. Then she unbuttoned his shirt and carefully pushed it off his shoulders and down his arms. She crouched before him to remove his shoes and socks and then pulled down his pants and underwear. Taking his hand, she led him to the extra-large tub they'd had installed to accommodate his size. He always took showers and couldn't remember the last time he'd taken a bath, but with bubbles filling the tub almost to the top and the scent of lavender, sage, and vanilla perfuming the air, the scene was very inviting.

"This smells good," he remarked.

"I found a bubble bath for men," Shanice said.

"You went through all of that trouble." He smiled at her.

She grinned, clearly pleased by his response. "It was no trouble. Get in." She slapped him on the ass and jumped back, giggling when he tried to grab her.

Cruz climbed in and settled into the warm water, and his body relaxed. Damn, he should do this more often.

"Good?" she asked, adjusting the bath pillow behind his back.

"Yes, but better if you joined me." His hungry gaze ate up the fullness of her figure in the dark khakis and cream top.

"The bath is for you. I want you to feel comfortable and relaxed."

"I'm most comfortable and relaxed when I'm with you. Come in and keep me company." He ran a hand up her pants leg, caressing her inner thigh.

"You want some of that sex now, huh?"

"Sex in the tub. That'll be new for us." Cruz wiggled his eyebrows.

"You wish, but I'll join you."

Shanice pulled the blouse over her head and let it fall to the floor. Cruz rested his arms on top of the tub, riveted by her strip-tease. When she was down to her panties, she turned her back and slowly moved the lace down her thighs, bending way over so her behind was in his face. He groaned and bit his bottom lip.

Straightening, she tossed a coquettish look over her shoulders. "You like what you see, *papi*? You want to spank my *culo*?" She wiggled her ass.

"I sure do, *mami*. Are you going to let me?"

"Are you sure you're up to it? With all those injuries—"

She let out a squeal as he surged to his feet and water sloshed over the side of the tub and splattered the tile. He lifted her into the tub and then carefully lowered them back into the water with her back against his chest.

"You were saying?"

"I made a mistake!" Shanice tossed back her head, letting out gut-busting laughter.

He squeezed her in his arms. It was nice to have someone he could enjoy himself with. They could make intense love but also laughed together.

When Shanice stopped laughing, Cruz moved his hands over her soft tummy and up to her breasts.

"I'm so glad you're home," she said in a quiet voice.

"Me, too." He kissed her ear and slid a hand between her thighs.

"Baby." Shanice moaned the endearment, moving in a sensual grind against him.

He played with her clit and rubbed the folds of her sex with his blunt fingers until her breathing changed into short, heavy draws of breath.

He licked and sucked on the side of her neck the way she liked and watched as she bent her knees and widened her legs. She pushed up into his hand, her dark nipples slipping above the sudsy water and teasing him. His left hand fondled her soft breasts and tweaked the tips into hard peaks.

"Cruz...*ohhh*." Hearing her moan like that set his blood ablaze.

Her body went rigid, and with a trembling cry she came, hips jerking spasmodically underwater.

Once her breathing went back to normal, Shanice sighed. "That was nice. You're next," she murmured.

"No, I just want to hold you for a little bit," Cruz said, much to the chagrin of his hard dick.

Although Shanice had spent a lot of time with him at the hospital, being in their own home without concern that medical personnel could interrupt them was the type of intimacy and togetherness he'd missed.

She stretched her left leg out of the sudsy water. "Mmm, that was really good. Welcome home, baby."

Cruz chuckled and pulled her earlobe between his teeth.

They sat quietly for several minutes before Shanice spoke again. "Do you think we're safe now? From Randall Logan, I mean."

He'd had plenty of time to think about the Logan situation while lying on his back at the clinic, and while he didn't want to scare Shanice, he didn't want to outright lie to her, either.

"Randall Logan still has a lot of power and influence, even while he's in jail. I don't think he's given up on me yet. He'll regroup and hire new men, so the only option is to stop him. Permanently."

"How do you plan to do that?" she asked in a hushed whisper.

"I'll think of something," Cruz replied, threading his fingers through hers.

"I'll let you handle that."

She wouldn't ask the details, and he wouldn't give her any. Violence had been a way of life for him long before they met. But he had a family now and had to be careful. He'd thought of a way to handle Randall Logan already, and soon he'd implement his plan.

Shanice turned her head toward him. "Kiss me."

He obliged, pressing his lips to her soft, sensual mouth and teasing her tongue with his.

Sighing softly, she settled against his chest. They ended up staying in the tub, talking and laughing, until the water became cold.

29

Shanice waited in the bedroom in her silk robe, seated on the side of the bed. Moist heat lay heavy between her legs as she anxiously waited for Cruz to finish up in the bathroom.

When he finally came out, she smiled seductively and called him over to the bed. As he watched her lower to her knees, a spark of lust nested in his eyes. She got rid of his towel and didn't waste any time taking his dick in her mouth and gently sucking the tip.

"Your mouth always feels so damn good," he whispered huskily, dark eyes focused on her actions as she swirled her tongue around his hard flesh, licking the seam and the underside.

She made sure to keep her mouth nice and wet and stroked her hands slowly up and down his thighs, scraping the insides with her nails.

His eyes narrowed to slits. "I'm gonna fuck that pretty mouth real good tonight."

His devilish promise turned her on even more, and she bobbed up and down his length, engulfing him deeper into her mouth each time. Cruz inhaled sharply and jerked, shoving his fingers into her hair. With a muttered Spanish curse, he slowly rotated his hips as he watched from above, nostrils flaring and eyes focused on the stretch of her lips around his hard flesh.

His breathing became more erratic, and the low sound of pleasure from his throat vibrated in her ears, a clear signal of his impending climax. She had him now. This big, strong man was under her control—at the mercy of her mouth.

Moaning and aroused by the act of submission to him, Shanice held his erection steady with one hand while the other played with her clit.

"I'm about to come," Cruz warned, eyes glittering down at her.

He didn't always come in her mouth. Sometimes he released on her chest or inside of her. Tonight, she signaled that she wanted him to finish in her mouth.

Shanice lifted her gaze to his and took him deeper, relaxing her throat muscles as the tip hit the back of her throat. He read the assent in her eyes and a muscle in his hard jaw twitched. His hand moved to her hair and tightened on the back of her head. When he thrust into her mouth, she groaned, focused on her breathing so she wouldn't gag. He pushed in over and over with abandon, yet she knew he was still holding back. His fingers were tight on her curls and his thigh muscles bulged from the effort of restraint.

When he finally released into her mouth, he bared his teeth as if the agony of release was almost too much to handle.

Shanice stood and kissed his heaving chest, letting her fingers caress the dark hairs sprinkled over his olive-toned skin. She ached for him. Her nipples were hard and between her legs wet and throbbing.

"On the bed," Cruz commanded.

Shanice fell onto the mattress and her silk robe flew partially open, exposing one thigh. She scooted backward and he followed her. He didn't bother untying her robe or making any attempt to undress her. He shoved the silky material up to her hips, his calloused hands gripping her knees as he pushed them open. Her skin flushed with the heat of anticipation. With her thighs spread open, he dived between her legs like a man at the end of his tether. The fact that he was so anxious to have her, didn't bother to waste time getting her undressed, fueled the flames of her desire and had her clutching his head as if she planned to absorb him into her own body.

He sucked and licked and ate her out with unfettered fervor, his hands keeping her legs open while he claimed every inch of her sex with his mouth and tongue. Almost immediately, her head tipped back and she fell over the edge into a mind-blowing orgasm that had her nails scraping the sheets and a hoarse, panting cry escaping her wide-open mouth.

As Shanice came back down to earth, Cruz climb on top of her. He was hard again, his jaw set in rigid, determined lines. Between her legs was damn near dripping from his merciless attention only seconds before, but clearly she wouldn't have much time to catch her breath because he was on a mission.

He pinched her nipples between his teeth and sucked them through the robe and she arched her spine. The smooth silk had become an unbearable barrier, seeming to chafe her skin as her breasts strained against the material in a need to get deeper into his mouth.

"I love to watch you come," Cruz whispered, fastening her wrists above her head with one hand. "Now I'm going to give you what you've been wanting all night."

He slid home with a throaty groan that reverberated from deep in his chest. Shanice cried out with satisfaction. He was right. This was exactly what she'd been craving. Her feminine muscles closed tight around him as if her sex had been formed with the exact dimensions to accommodate his dick.

As he thrust deep inside her trembling core, Shanice

moaned in frustration. She both hated and loved this position. Hated it because she couldn't touch him. Loved it because being under his control heightened her arousal as she immersed herself in the sensation of his body dominating hers.

His other hand came up to her throat and squeezed, firm but gentle as it limited her supply of oxygen. This feeling of powerlessness, of giving him complete control, only ratcheted up her arousal. Light-headed as endorphins surged through her body, Shanice's eyes rolled back in her head, and her mouth fell open, eyes glazing over as she lost focus on the room.

She could hardly breathe and was completely helpless— her arms pinned to the bed, his hand at her throat, and his thrusting hips relentlessly hitting right every time.

Shanice couldn't focus on anything else but the way he controlled her. The way he made her feel. Alive. Aroused. Out of control.

"*Tu eres mi alma gemela, mami,*" Cruz said to her in a rough whisper. "*Mi tesoro. Mi vida.*" You're my soulmate. My sweetheart. My life.

Those romantic words had barely left his lips when another orgasm slowly unfurled in her loins.

"Baby," she whispered in his ear. "Yes, yes."

The panted words riled him up more and he thrust harder with firm, short strokes.

Shanice pressed her heels into his lower back, taking him as deep as he could go.

She came hard, grimacing under the force of her climax. Reeling with the throes of ecstasy, she yelled his name. "I'm coming again, I'm coming again, I'm coming...!"

Her fingers and toes curled tight as wave after wave of climactic sensations washed through her and rocked her body with delicious tremors.

Cruz came soon after, his fingers tightening around her

bound wrists, his other hand gripping her right hip as he guided his hard flesh repeatedly into the slickness at the apex of her thighs.

Afterward, exhausted, they managed to drag their bodies higher on the bed and settled on the pillows. Shanice rolled immediately into his arms.

THEY HADN'T BOTHERED to pull up the sheets around them. Cruz remained naked and Shanice's robe was twisted around her waist. The room air cooled her exposed bottom, but she didn't care. She was still reliving the intensity of their love-making moments before and didn't want to move. Didn't want to let go of him.

She pressed her nose to his neck and deeply inhaled. Musky from a day's work or freshly showered, she loved to smell him. Right now, her nostrils filled with his male scent and the soothing aroma of lavender and sage.

Shanice smiled sleepily as Cruz drew her closer.

"I'm gonna sleep like a baby now," she murmured.

"Me, too. Better than I did in that hospital." He gently rubbed up and down her back.

"I was thinking about something. I'm going to stop taking the pill. I'm ready to have another baby. Is that okay with you?"

"Of course."

He'd wanted to expand their family right away, but she'd wanted to wait a while since they were newly married and he was working on his business. They were settled now, and though she was about to open the bookstore, her mother would be there to help. They discussed their options while he was in the hospital, and Cruz suggested that they turn the pool house into an in-law suite for Miriam. Shanice loved the idea because her mother would be close but still be able to maintain her privacy.

"We can have the last two closer together. What do you think?" Cruz asked.

"I was thinking the same thing. No more than two years apart."

"Agreed."

Shanice ran a hand up and down his chest and let her fingers idle in his springy chest hairs.

"I know the past week has been rough," Cruz said thoughtfully. "Are you okay?"

Shanice flung a leg across his and nodded. "I'm fine now. I got what I wanted. You're home."

hy am I here?

W There was nothing Miles had to say that Cruz should be listening to, yet here he was, seated in a chair in front of his desk because Miles said he had something important he needed to speak to Cruz about in person.

He glanced around Miles's new office. It was larger than his old one, decorated in brown and tan colors, with a view of the street through the blinds covering the one window. On the walls were awards he'd received over the years for his work in the government, and on the desk two photos of his daughter— one showing her as a newborn and the other showing her first day of kindergarten. In a few years, Cruz and Shanice would be taking a similar photo of Alex.

The door behind him opened and closed, and Miles entered. "Sorry to keep you waiting." He dropped some papers on his desk. "Glad you could come."

"What's this about?"

Miles chuckled. "Cut to the chase, as always. Okay, I hear you. Last month I was pulled into a high-level meeting at the White House. Shocked the hell out of me, but turns out our new President and his advisors heard about the "special agency" I used to work in. Long story short, Plan B is being reborn under the Office for Targeted Violence and Terrorism Prevention, and I'm the new director."

His declaration stunned Cruz. "Wow. Congratulations."

"And I want you to come back."

Cruz stood.

Miles put up his hands to stop him. "Wait a minute, don't leave! Hear me out. Don't tell me you didn't get excited during that rescue operation in Tennessee."

"I was rescuing my *kid*," Cruz reminded him.

"You're bored guarding those rich people and performing background checks on their enemies."

"Says who?"

"I know you, Cruz. Being a bodyguard is not enough."

Miles went over to the bar. A bar in his office was new. His new position had its privileges. He poured himself two fingers of Scotch.

"Let me have one of those," Cruz said.

"Sure." Miles handed over his glass and poured himself another.

Cruz took a sip. "Shanice would never approve of me coming back."

"Then don't tell her," Miles said nonchalantly, as if deceiving his wife was no big deal.

His suggestion was tempting, but Cruz shook his head. "I can't do that."

"Give her a baby then. That'll keep her busy."

"I want another kid, but what kind of solution is that? That's some shitty advice."

Miles shrugged. "My father told me that. He always gave the best worst advice. His theory was that one kid wasn't enough to keep a woman tied to you through the bad times, but give her two or more, and you pretty much have her locked in." He stared down into his Scotch. "I guess it worked, in his case. My mother wouldn't leave him, no matter how many times he hit her, and when he finally died, she actually cried."

Miles had had a complicated relationship with his father before he died. After he became an adult and graduated from college, he tried to get his mother to leave his father, but she refused because by then he'd become ill and couldn't take care of himself. She felt obligated to help him, despite all he'd done to her—broken bones, bruises, black eyes. She couldn't walk away, even after the opportunity presented itself.

"To be honest, I'm pretty sure you could tell Shanice because frankly, she knows the man she married. The fight is in your blood, and you're damn good at what you do."

"What exactly are you offering?"

Miles smiled knowingly.

"I haven't said I'll come back. I'm curious," Cruz said.

"Right, right." Miles smirked and stepped back over to the desk, where he rested a hip. "Whether you're part of the organization or not, Plan B is going to happen, but I'd rather have you involved. The President wants a small team of specialists—people with surgical skill who can get the job done—here and abroad—with limited blow back. No need for a cleaver when a scalpel will do. Basically, what you used to do, except this time I'll be in charge, and I have an indirect line to the President through the National Security Advisor. I want you to build the team, but this time you'll be contractors instead of employees, so the money is better."

He'd have input into building the team. That part was definitely intriguing. Cruz's mind raced with the possibilities.

"So I recruit the agents, and you hire the Cordoba Agency?"

"Exactly, and the Cordoba Agency is the perfect cover. Your Plan B staff will be able to travel around without generating suspicion."

"And if anything goes wrong...?"

"That remains the same, of course. Anything goes wrong, you're on your own. I'm simply an assistant director at Homeland Security, and the U.S. government doesn't know anything about you or what you're up to. As far as we know, Cruz Cordoba runs a security firm."

Cruz paced away from him. Deep in thought, he took a sip of the Scotch and swung back around. "You're going to pay out the nose."

Miles laughed. "I already figured that. The money's there, believe me. Domestic terrorism is on the rise and the FBI is overwhelmed with white supremacists and other extremists. By the way, I have a bit of information you'll be interested in. Since I've been here, I did some poking around, trying to learn more about Nancy's death. Nothing official, strictly on my own time. I found out she was friends with J.C.'s mother. After his parents died, she looked out for him."

"That was sloppy of Nancy to hire someone she knew."

Miles nodded his agreement. "Very. The question is, why would she? Which leads me to my next bit of news. I told the President about my suspicions concerning Nancy—that I didn't think she committed suicide. He wants me to open a full investigation into her death. If you come on board, that's the first case we'll be working on."

Looking into Nancy's death was definitely of interest to Cruz, especially now that he knew about the J.C. connection. As a bonus, working with Miles in this new capacity could set the Cordoba Agency apart from other agencies. He'd have access to information and resources other security companies didn't, which could place them in the top tier and able to charge a higher premium.

"There are people out there who want to hurt our country in all kinds of ways, including take down the government, and the President wants to cut them down before they do major damage. Pull your team together and name your price, and I'll present the budget."

This was an interesting proposition, but he needed time to think about the offer. "I'll let you know something soon."

"Is that a yes?"

"That's an 'I'll let you know something soon.'"

"I'll be waiting." Miles looked very satisfied, as if he already knew what Cruz's answer would be.

Cruz knew what he himself wanted. He could already feel his blood pumping and a general sense of excitement under his skin, but he couldn't make this decision in a vacuum. He had a wife he needed to discuss the idea with.

He set down the empty glass and headed to the door. "I'll be in touch."

31

C ruz watched as Randall Logan entered the room with
a guard. Behind the Plexiglass, the old man shuffled
in wearing an orange jumpsuit and leaning heavily
on his cane. His shoulders were more stooped than when Cruz
had seen him on the news four years ago. When he looked at
Cruz behind his thick glasses, he didn't seem surprised.

Cruz picked up the phone on his side and so did Randall.
Neither said a word. They simply stared at each other, two
enemies facing off in silence.

"What are you doing here?" Randall finally asked.

"Who told you where to find me?" Cruz asked.

Randall's twisted smile looked more like a sneer. "Wouldn't
you like to know, but I won't tell you. Just know that I'll pull
together an even bigger army next time. I won't rest until I've
killed you."

"Be careful, they record these conversations."

"I don't give a damn!" Randall's eyes flashed with the thirst
for revenge.

"Who told you where to find me?"

Randall laughed, an evil maniacal laugh that demonstrated

how much hate consumed him. "Go to hell." He leaned closer to the glass. "And watch your back."

"Be concerned about yourself, old man. You're in here with a bunch of hardened criminals and can barely walk."

Randall laughed. "You can't touch me in here."

"Never said I would, but anything can happen in a place like this." Cruz knew better than to make an outright threat.

"What do you plan to do? Get yourself arrested so you can come in here and kill me yourself?"

Cruz laughed. "Much as I'd like to gut you like a fish, you give me too much credit, and you're not worth the loss of my freedom, especially since I have a family now. But strange things have been known to happen behind prison walls. Some men can't take the stress and commit suicide." He stared into Randall's eyes, telepathing the message about the "suicide" he'd orchestrated after Shanice's journalist friend uncovered Randall's illegal dealings.

The old man's eyes flickered with doubt for a moment, and then his face creased into a feral smile.

"You don't have the kind of money I do, and I'm a god in here. My bodyguards have bodyguards. My protection is impenetrable, and there's not an inmate in here willing to touch me because he knows he'll be risking his life."

It was Cruz's turned to sneer, and he placed his face closer to the glass. "I don't care what you have, old man. You threatened my family and now you're threatening my life. Watch *your* back. For karma's sake, I mean. Karma's a bitch. Say your prayers and hope there's a god willing to listen and forgive your sins and not smite you down with his mighty fist. The way he did your son."

A light of rage jumped to life in Randall's eyes. "Y-you're a dead man," he sputtered. "Your whole family is dead, do you hear me? Dead!" Randall slammed down the phone and struggled up from the chair. He was shaking with anger, eyes trained on Cruz as if he considered breaking through the glass and choking the life out of him.

The guard led him away and Cruz finally stood, thoughts already going to next steps of activating the contact Raheem had uncovered at the prison.

Kill before you're killed. That's what he'd been taught in Plan B. As long as Randall Logan was alive, the violence wouldn't end. Looking over his shoulder wouldn't end. His family would never be safe.

So he had no choice but to take the old man's life.

RANDALL LOGAN SHUFFLED into the bathroom with shower shoes and his soap and towel, a pair of boxers hanging low on his hips. Now was the best time to take a shower because the bathroom was usually empty this time of day. He could only hear one other person, and they were all the way down at the end.

He'd been in this hell hole for three years and still hadn't gotten used to the very basic nature of the showers. He missed his sauna, rainfall showerhead, and ability to adjust the water temperature, and it grieved him that he could no longer pipe in the soothing sounds of classical music.

At least this prison had stalls, and he didn't have to suffer through a community shower like he'd seen portrayed so many times in the movies. He set his cane inside the stall and pulled closed the curtain. When he pushed down the loose-fitting boxers, they landed around his ankles. Completely removing them would take too much effort, so he left them alone and turned on the water. Lukewarm spray hit his shoulders and dribbled down his chest and back. They still hadn't fixed the water heater! His aching muscles and arthritic joints missed the soothing balm of a hot shower.

His conversation with Cruz Cordoba yesterday still had him agitated, but before long he'd figure out a way to make that filthy Cuban pay. No price was too high to get rid of him. He'd have his whole house burned down with his family in it, if he had to.

He heard the door open and close but continued lathering soap on his chest, his thoughts on the planned destruction of the man who'd murdered his son.

He heard voices and the shower at the other end stopped, and then the room became eerily quiet except for the running of his own faucet. His curtain was pulled across, and Randall swung his head around to see who'd dared interrupt his private moment.

Richter, one of the guards, stood behind him. A large, bald Black man, he'd only seen him a few times.

"What do you want?" Randall asked rudely. He wasn't a common prisoner. He paid dearly for the privilege to be left alone and treated better than the others.

"I have a message for you."

The guard's heavy voice sounded like an ominous warning and caused a frisson of fear to race down Randall's back. Turning awkwardly because of his physical limitations and the boxers around his feet, Randall fully faced the man, his gaze climbing up his chest to dark eyes filled with malevolent intent.

"You should have never fucked with me," the guard said.

Randall opened his mouth to scream but was too late. Richter jammed a shiv below the ribs and into the soft tissue of his stomach.

As pain ripped through him, Randall staggered back and hit the wall. The guard yanked the weapon from the wound, and Randall watched in silent horror as his life's blood poured out and reddened the water running into the drain.

The weapon was simply a toothbrush with the handle sharpened to a point, which Richter lifted high and dropped with force into the side of Randall's neck, before yanking it right back out again. Excruciating pain wracked his weakened body as he fell hard and his head hit the side of the cement stall divider. With his mouth frozen open from the searing pain, only a hoarse moan escaped his vocal chords.

Before his eyes closed, he watched more blood ooze down the drain, and his last thought was one of regret.

He should have never fucked with Cruz Cordoba.

———

32

"You haven't been the same since you came back from your visit with Miles," Shanice observed.

They were seated next to the pool on a cushioned bench, and Shanice had her feet in his lap. In her hand was a glass of sweet iced tea, and Cruz held a bottle of beer.

"We had an interesting conversation," he admitted.

"What about?" She sipped her iced tea.

"Stuff." He was still figuring out how to broach the subject of the reincarnated version of Plan B.

"What kind of stuff, Cruz?"

"Nothing to worry your head about. I'm still sorting it out." He patted her calf.

"I think it's very noble that you want to protect me, but we're married, and we're partners. I understand your need for discretion with work-related issues, but I don't appreciate you keeping non-work related secrets from me."

"What makes you think I'm keeping secrets from you?"

She arched an eyebrow. "Because I know you, and I know when it's personal. When it's work-related, you'll share what you can without breaking client confidentiality. When it's personal, you don't share at all."

He chuckled and squeezed one of her feet. She'd recently painted her toes a bright red, and he liked the color on her. "You know me well."

"I've learned a thing or two being married to you. I look for patterns." The soft smile on her face died. "What's wrong, babe?"

He heaved a sigh and rubbed his thumb into her insole and then stopped.

"The Plan B program has been revived, and Miles is the new director. He wants me to come back and help him build a team."

"Oh." She swallowed. "What about the Cordoba Agency?"

"It would still be in business and would provide a cover for the Plan B missions when the government contracts the work to us. Essentially, the U.S. government will be one of our clients." He watched her closely to gauge her reaction.

Shanice took another sip of tea and then cradled the glass in both hands. "So you'd be going back into the field?"

"Yes."

"What happens when you have to go deep under cover?"

"I won't accept any of those assignments for myself." That was a decision he'd made on his own. He didn't want to leave her wondering, and he couldn't stand the thought of being away from her and Alex with no communication between them. That worked fine when he was alone, but those days were long gone.

She looked down into the brown liquid and asked quietly, "What do you want to do?"

"I promised you I would walk away from that life."

She looked up at him. "But what do you *want* to do?"

He didn't respond, and the silence stretched between them,

filled only by the nighttime sounds. Finally, she looked away into the darkness.

"I'm not going to do it," Cruz said. He couldn't, wouldn't disappoint her and disrupt the life they'd created together.

Shanice shook her head and looked at him. "You have to."

"No, I don't."

"Yes, you do," she insisted.

Cruz drained the beer and set down the empty bottle. "No, I don't. Look, I made you a promise, and I intend to keep it. We have a son, and soon we'll be giving him more siblings, right?" He flashed a smile, and she responded with one of her own. "Eight to five, like I promised."

Shanice dropped her feet to the ground and took his hand in hers. Her fingers were so soft and smooth compared to his.

"Yes, you made me a promise, but I shouldn't have asked that of you in the first place. At the time, I was emotional. Being pregnant probably didn't help, I don't know. But I'm setting you free from that promise."

"No, Shanice. I—"

"*Yes*, Cruz." She smiled at him and squeezed his hand between both of hers. "My dad used to say that everyone has purpose, and they have to use their talents to accomplish their purpose. I believe your purpose is to improve our society, improve our country. I appreciate you wanting to keep your promise to me, I really do. But that was a selfish request on my part. I want you to myself 365 days a year. I want to know with a little bit of confidence that you'll always come back to us. But that's my needs. If you were a businessman or a lawyer or a plumber, there's no guarantee that you'll come home to us every day because accidents happen.

"But, babe, I don't think you're more likely to die than someone in any of the professions I mentioned. Your desire to do the right thing, to help people, to protect our country and our way of life...that's who you are. I don't want to stifle that. And you're so freaking good at what you do, that even though I know you enjoy your work at the Cordoba Agency, I also know it's not enough. The same way staying at home wasn't enough for me. But we came to an agreement, and soon I'll have my own bookstore."

They'd talked in depth about the store, and her mother coming to stay with them was the right solution that allowed Shanice to move forward. Miriam could be close to her family but have her own privacy in the in-law suite, and Cruz would have peace of mind knowing someone trustworthy was taking care of their son.

"Plan B is really where your heart is, and I understand that. And I'm glad you'll be able to participate on your own terms this time. So that's that. Tell Miles you accept the offer, and no arguing with me about your decision anymore." She released his hand and sat back.

"You're really okay with this?"

He didn't want to cause her grief or worry, but excitement was already building in his chest. His conversation with Miles had triggered ideas and thoughts about how he could reshape Plan B. He already knew who he'd recruit—the same people who'd helped him rescue his son were at the top of the list.

"Just promise me one thing." She laughed. "Sorry, more promises."

"Anything."

She sobered. "Come back to us. Every time."

"I will. I promise," Cruz said.

But they both knew there was no guarantee, and his promise was as empty as the beer bottle on the ground, but his response wasn't about truth. Those words were meant to allay any remnants of fear and ensure she knew he would never put himself at unnecessary risk because he had a family—people who loved and cared about him and were waiting for his return.

Shanice wound her arms around his chest. "Love you."

She was so generous with affection and always said "I love you." She was open and loving, with words and in actions. She made it easier for him to receive and show affection in return.

The other day he'd looked up his aunt and uncle in Miami and planned to give them a call in the next day or two, to reopen the lines of communication. The old Cruz would have never done that. The old Cruz had written them off the same way they had him. But thanks to Shanice, he was willing to reach out. He was no longer just an emotionless automaton trained to kill. Now he was a loving family man who looked forward to re-establishing a relationship with his aunt and uncle. She had no idea how much she'd changed him.

"Love you, too, *mami*," he whispered. He tasted her soft mouth and tugged her bottom lip between his teeth.

The back door opened and Alex trudged out with Mr. Cuddles in a one-armed headlock.

"Hey, what are you doing up?" Shanice lifted him onto her lap, and he mumbled something unintelligible as he rested his cheek on her breasts.

His son's dark gaze met his for a second before Alex's eyes drooped closed.

"Out like a light," Cruz whispered, running a hand over his son's curly hair.

Then he stretched his arm along the back of the bench and around Shanice's shoulders. He listened to her humming to Alex as his gaze encompassed the back yard, the pool house, and the dark water shimmering under the moonlight.

This was his family, his reason for living. No one had ever meant as much to him as these two people. And he made a promise to himself as they sat out there and he listened to his wife hum a melody as she gently rocked their son.

He would keep his promise to Shanice. No matter the operation, no matter where he was sent in the country or the world —he would always come back to them.

Every time.

BONUS CONTENT

If you enjoyed this story, join my mailing list to read deleted scenes of Cruz and Shanice before and on their wedding day!

Use the QR code or enter the link below in your browser.

geni.us/DDBonusContent

ALSO BY DELANEY DIAMOND

More books in The Cordoba Agency series!

Until Now (The Cordoba Agency #1)

For Cruz Cordoba, a simple off-the-books assignment becomes a race of life and death.

Until Death (The Cordoba Agency #2)

The best laid plans can still go awry . . . in the most terrifying way. Read the exciting conclusion to Cruz and Shanice's love story.

Heart Stealer (The Cordoba Agency #3)

Katherine was older, sophisticated, and years ago she broke Raheem's heart. Now he must keep her alive and his desire in check. Easier said than done.

Almost Perfect (The Cordoba Agency #4)

A cat burglar and an assassin run for their lives across Paris—and try not to get distracted by the sizzling attraction between them.

Forever Again (The Cordoba Agency #5)

To get a second chance at love, two assassins must survive a criminal enterprise determined to wreak havoc in America's Paradise.

Audiobook samples, free short stories, and the full catalogue of her books are available at www.delaneydiamond.com.

ABOUT THE AUTHOR

Delaney Diamond is the USA Today Bestselling Author of sensual, passionate romance novels. Originally from the U.S. Virgin Islands, she now lives in Atlanta, Georgia. She reads romance novels, mysteries, thrillers, and a fair amount of nonfiction. When she's not busy reading or writing, she's in the kitchen trying out new recipes, dining at one of her favorite restaurants, or traveling to an interesting locale.

Enjoy free reads on her website. Join her mailing list to get sneak peeks, notices of sale prices, and find out about new releases.

Join her mailing list
www.delaneydiamond.com

f facebook.com/DelaneyDiamond
instagram.com/delaneydiamondbooks
X x.com/DelaneyDiamond
pinterest.com/delaneydiamond

www.ingramcontent.com/pod-product-compliance
Lightning Source LLC
Chambersburg PA
CBHW070008260626
47159CB00005B/1727